Florence Crannell Means

1963

HOUGHTON MIFFLIN COMPANY BOSTON

The Riverside Press Cambridge

To

Mather School

which has been lighting

candles with selfless

devotion since

1867

1

Commencement Day!

Jane Emmeline Tolliver, Tolly for short, breathed deep of the sunny June morning. She drew her slim five feet six even taller, as if she were about to take flight into the bright sky. She laughed aloud with the beauty of the Tennessee day, and the joy that brimmed and spilled over within her.

"Oh, what a beautiful morning!" she sang in her throaty contralto. "Everything's going my way."

Everything was: fulfillment almost too many-sided and complete. She was to be graduated from Fisk today, but that was only part of it. She would also be cited as newly initiated Phi Beta Kappa and awarded a *magna cum laude*. And she was only nineteen.

Yesterday had been the baccalaureate, with her father pronouncing the benediction. He was as proud and happy as she, and so was her mother, and — as far as a twelve-year-old imp of a boy could be impressed by such adult matters — so was her brother Dabney, over at one of the guest houses now, with her parents. So was her younger sister Ellen, a freshman here at Fisk, who, like all the others, had had to vacate her dormitory room for parents and friends of the graduates.

"Everything's going my way!" Tolly repeated, her happiness bubbling still higher.

For something besides commencement and honors was coming. Sojer was approaching her across the campus, his left arm swinging as it always did, purposefully, as if to sweep any obstacles from his path.

"But why does he walk so slow?" Tolly wondered, half aloud. Her tone and expression were indulgently concerned. She had toiled so ceaselessly to help him through the premed course here at Fisk that she combined the pride and anxiety of mother, teacher, sculptor.

Sojourner Truth Pratt had enjoyed none of Tolly's advantages. She had been born on St. Helena Island, to educated parents, her father a minister and her mother a teacher. Sojer was a native of the Black Belt of Virginia, his father and mother almost illiterate, and his early rural schooling in rickety shacks, taught by women who had at best passed the eighth grade in schools no better than his.

Watching him approach, Tolly wondered how ambition had been kindled to so fierce a flame in the child Sojer, and against his father's bitter opposition. His mother, Tolly knew, had bent her back over white women's washtubs, and chopped and picked cotton in season, so that her eldest son could set aside his earnings for school.

He had been a sort of dark-skinned Abraham Lincoln, lying prone on the clay hearth of the cabin, poring over a book by firelight when the kerosene was used up. He had worked at every kind of rough, heavy job to get to Fisk, and it had seemed a miracle to him when he was actually there.

But the four college years had been the hardest of all, and without Tolly's help he could never have passed them.

"You have a superior mind, Pratt," one of his teachers had said. "With that mind and your dedication, you could be a power among your people in almost any profession. But you have to face it — your preliminary education is a fearful handicap."

For a while this spring he and Tolly had both thought the handicap too great. But here he was, and it was Commencement Day, and next fall he would enroll in Meharry Medical School, across from the campus. Though he and Tolly had not quite "gone steady," it was taken for granted that they would keep on working together, she teaching until he was established as a physician. That future represented the brightest glory of Tolly's day.

Nothing less, she thought, would have made up for the time she had given, foregoing all the "fun things" of college, which she had looked forward to from her childhood. Sometimes during these years Tolly had cried over missing so much. But once she set her strong little chin to push and pull Sojer through, she could not be satisfied by doing a halfway job.

And now Sojer, though his pace was so strangely slow, was near enough so that she could see his fine head, set on the strong neck with the beauty of poise that seemed peculiar to well-built Negro youth. He was not handsome — he always said Tolly was handsome enough for two — but he was good to look at, his eyebrows shooting up and out strongly above the steady brown eyes, and the mouth folded so straight when it was not flashing open over white teeth. Sojourner Truth. The name fitted, even though it had first belonged to a woman, one of the strongest leaders of their people.

Tolly smiled her own big, shining smile as he drew near. Usually it lighted his, but not today.

"Tolly," he said when he was close enough, "can you take time to go some'rs and talk a little? The Browsing Room, maybe. My folks are yonder at Jubilee, and —"

Then it must be his parents he was troubled about — his father. "Why, yes, if we make haste," Tolly agreed, "but the Browsing Room is closed in the morning."

"Open on Commencement Day," he said. "So folks can see it."

She followed him toward the stately pile of the library, and they hurried through the impressive oak-paneled lobby and up the flights of stairs to the Browsing Room. Here they would not be disturbed.

They pushed through to a far corner, behind the grand piano, and sat down opposite each other at a small table.

"How do you like the new way I've done my hair?"

4

Tolly asked, trying to coax a smile to the disturbing somberness of Sojer's face.

He barely glanced at the clusters of glossy black curls over her forehead. "You ever beautiful," he said, but as if he were sorry rather than glad.

"Beautiful?" Tolly scoffed. "With such a big mouth?"

Ordinarily he would have looked at her with the wondering admiration she loved, and said something about its being just right. "Any littler," he had assured her the other day, "and it couldn't shout the spirituals the way it does with the University Choir. Tolly, you just a brown satin angel with two black stars for eyes. And a beautiful long neck full of singing."

Today he said nothing like this, and Tolly felt a chill draft quenching her happiness. She glanced toward the window. Surely a cloud had hidden the sun.

"Well, for goodness' sake," Tolly cried, but her protest broke off as she looked at Sojer.

He had forgotten the newly acquired nicety of pulling out her chair for her, and had dropped down and folded his big, workworn hands before him. He was gazing at Tolly as if he could hardly bear to look or not to look; gazing as if he were trying to print her face indelibly on his mind.

"Why — Sojer!" Tolly breathed protestingly. She wondered whether his father's savage temper had exploded into violence. Or whether seeing his parents after a separation had made the gulf between him and Tolly seem too great. But, no, they had agreed that

5

Sojer's background must remain his background, and that he must stand on his own achievement.

He lifted one of those calloused hands with the immensely long, square-tipped fingers that Tolly thought were certainly a surgeon's hands. He lifted it to silence her.

"Wait, girl. Wait twell I tell you. But however I gwine say it?" he groaned.

She stared at him, frightened by his intensity.

"Those finals," he said huskily, "the three in my toughest courses —" again a struggling stillness — "The German and the chemistry —"

"But, Sojer! You came through all three with the highest marks you've ever had — higher than in your easy subjects."

Once more the long hand silenced her. "My adviser, he tell me it all depend on my finals. My classwork wasn't up to the grade." Now the words burst from him as if they tore him apart. "Tolly, I keep thinking about you: Early Entrant and Phi Beta and *cum laude* and all. And all along I think you won't be ashamed of me when I'm Dr. Pratt. And — next — I think about our own people, and helping them like I dream since I was a little child. It seemed like nothing could be more wrong than to — oh, Tolly, to fail them — and fail you."

"But —" Tolly's voice was bewildered.

"Tolly, I cheated in those three finals," he rushed on. "Fellow had some papers he plan to use. Don't know how he got them. Well, I learned them by heart. Made

6

notes on my shirt tail, likewise."

Tolly moistened her lips. "Sojer, no," she whispered. "Not you. I don't believe it."

He was gazing at her as if she might be snatched away at any minute. "I done it — me, Sojourner Truth. It look like the onliest thing to do." — How his old way of speech came back in his anguish — "Like sneaking a loaf of bread efn yo' mam was starving —"

"That's exactly it!" Tolly spoke on a swiftly indrawn breath, and a hot wave of anger swept her, anger for Sojer. "It wasn't your fault. It was those white folks that paid you no mind. How much they spend for each Negro child's education? Seems like it's four dollars a year. That's why school integration comes so hard: the poor children never had a chance. Oh, Sojer, I hate them for it."

The face opposite her was even more solemn. "We got no right to hate. Not even white folks. Our South is poor. The white chillen here don't get much more chance than us —"

"Sojer," she cried, still strong with wrath at the white people and their system, "I know just how bad you feel. You're so honest. It doesn't matter to you that hundreds of students are cheating and thinking nothing of it. And you're right to feel that way. But now you've got to go ahead and forget it. The good Lord wouldn't have let you get through if He hadn't meant you to go on," she insisted when he made no response. "And you can make up for it by the way you serve our people."

7

"Girl, you don't understand." He was shaking his head as he whispered the words. "The Lord, He didn't let me get through. He stopped me in my tracks."

She stared at him with dawning comprehension. "You mean — they know?"

"That's right. The exams were too good to be true, and they run it all down. Didn't catch the child that gave 'em to me and use'm hisself. But they catch me. Sent for me late last night —"

"You mean — ?" she repeated.

"I'm not graduating. I'm through. Finished."

2

Tolly felt the blood drain from her face, leaving it stiff and cold. She stared at the wan grayness of Sojer and then stared past him.

"Not graduating? I don't believe it," she whispered. "Not after the years of work —"

She meant his own work and his mother's, of course. But her own part grew upon her, the work that had cost her so much gay young fun. No, she couldn't go to the picnic: she had to coach Sojer. She couldn't take time for the dance: she must go over Sojer's term paper with him. Always she must help bridge the gap between his early lack of education and the requirements of a college like this.

The blood flooded back into her face, up to her hairline. She had overlooked Sojer's uncouthness, thinking she saw the high potential under it. Some of her flippant classmates had poked fun at him, and consequently at her. The more sympathetic ones could see the splendid future that Tolly had been counting on a brief half-hour ago, with Sojer a physician and Tolly a teacher, and both working in a big way for their people.

And they had both taken a stand for the old-fashioned

virtues, honesty, purity, courage. She could imagine the mocking laughter of some of her classmates when they heard that the "holier than thou" Sojer had been dropped for cheating. He was too honest even to cheat skillfully, and the thought made her anger grow. They would pity her, Tolly, for having backed a loser and she hated pity.

The steadiness of his gaze drew hers back to him. "Looks like they's some truth in what they say. Ain't so bad to do wrong, but sho' a crime to get caught."

That was too near her thoughts. For a moment the raw pain in his voice jerked her back from her own injury to his tragedy. She stared at the lines that furrowed his fine forehead, at his drawn face. Overnight it had grown gaunt.

"Your father and mother," she remembered. "How did they take it?"

"They was plumb wore out and asleep before I knew. I told them to meet me in the Jubilee pa'lor this morning."

"They don't know? They think you're being graduated?"

"That's right. I rather be frailed then tell 'em. Pa might haul off and wallop me at that. But it's Ma —" He widened his eyes, swallowing desperately — "Tolly, you wouldn't go along whilst I tell 'em?"

Though Tolly's whole self revolted at the ordeal, she could not resist the humble pleading of his gaze. Abruptly she nodded and got up. "I told Papa and

Mama that I'd be over at eight, and it's already half past. Maybe we'd better — better break the news to them and then go on to Jubilee."

At the guest house they found the senior Tollivers and Ellen in the lounge waiting. Dabney, they said, was prowling round the campus. Though Mr. Tolliver's voice had a suggestion of the ministerial tone, and his manner a suggestion of the delivery of an important speech, his was nevertheless a welcoming warmth that showed his liking for Sojer. One got used to the pulpit tone, just as one got used to the gold in his teeth, so that they did not detract from the good smile in his round face.

Mrs. Tolliver, as tall as Tolly, and with the freckles and gray eyes she had passed on to her son but not to her daughters, gave a small, stiff bow. She had never been sure she approved of this young man's homespun qualities. Tolly could have got all wool with a finer finish.

Sixteen-year-old Ellen smiled deliciously, as she did at every nice boy.

Automatically, Tolly fastened Ellen's blouse one button higher and whispered, "Too much lipstick, lambie. Too much rouge." She had always thought that no other girl was so lusciously pretty as Ellen. A good half-head shorter than Tolly, she was all warm curves and dimples. Tolly adored her and worried over her and tried her best to make her act like a lady.

But this morning Sojer was her concern.

"You know where you go for the exercises?" she needlessly asked her parents. "Or Ellen can tell you. I've got to be ready in about a half-hour —"

"And Sojer likewise," her father agreed, tipping from his heels to his toes and back and contemplating them benignly.

Sojer gulped and stared at his clasped hands.

Tolly spoke hurriedly. "Well — no. Something has come up. Sojer isn't getting his diploma. Not today. Come on, Sojer, we've got to make tracks."

"Not getting his diploma? What on earth?" Ellen babbled, while the other two stood dumfounded.

"Tell you later," Tolly called back, already on her way. "We've got to go to Mr. and Mrs. Pratt — at Jubilee. They don't know yet."

"Just a minute!" Mrs. Tolliver's command halted their headlong retreat. "Won't this be a frightful shock? And when they've come so far?"

When neither Tolly nor Sojer made the obvious answer, she added, as if native kindness overcame her social standards, "Sojer, we'd be pleased if they'd have dinner with us after the exercises. You, too, of course."

"Thank you kindly, ma'am." Sojer gave a little jerk of head and foot. "I tell them. But I reckon they — we all — head straight for home."

Once outside the guest house both young people sighed with relief, though they knew the harder part was to come. "But we have to make haste," Tolly reminded both Sojer and herself.

"Take our foot in our hand," he mechanically agreed, lengthening his long stride.

Crossing the campus, they exchanged greetings with many fellow students, singly and in groups. None of them knew yet, Tolly thought, glancing at them sharply. They'd hear soon enough.

Around the Oval they sprinted, and up the steps of old Victorian Jubilee. The lounge they entered was quaintly impressive, its high windows deep embrasured, its staircase sweeping downward with a grand flourish. Here the waiting Pratts sat stiffly, eyes straight ahead. Their faces lightened as the young people approached, Sojer ducking a bow.

"A good morning to you," he said politely. "I hope you rested good after your hard trip. May I present Miss Tolliver? She the one I tell you about — Tolly," he added with unhappy pride.

While all four bowed, nodded, murmured, Tolly was studying the two. Though she had never before seen them, they did not surprise her, for she had braced herself for shabbiness and awkwardness.

Her glance did flit past them to another waiting couple, registering the contrast as they exchanged smiling salutations with her. They were the Todhunters, parents of Langston, whom she had sometimes dated. Mr. Todhunter was sleekly smooth, with a carefully clipped small mustache, and slacks and sport coat expensively casual. Mrs. Todhunter wore a hat that looked like tomorrow, shoes delicately perfect, a glint of diamonds on manicured hands.

Sojer's father was almost as tall as his son, but there the likeness ended. One didn't see many of her people who looked cross, Tolly thought, but Mr. Pratt's ruggedly hewn, pockmarked face was twisted fiercely, as if he had just drunk a bitter tea. His body seemed as unhappy as his face. His shirt collar poked up above a coat collar that dipped backward, and coarse cuffs protruded from coat sleeves a little too short.

Sojer's mother was as shabby. She was much shorter than her husband, with shoulders so rounded and chest so flattened that she might almost be turned front hindmost. Tolly knew enough to guess that hers was the shapelessness of incessant toil, starchy foods, and childbearing without care. It was evident that she had tried to make herself respectable for a great occasion, the occasion of a lifetime. The sleazy, styleless dress, the shoes that could not hide the spread distortion of the feet, the ridiculous hat perched above her weary face, all were new.

Tolly lingered over that weary face. Unlike Sojer in other ways, his mother met the girl's gaze with eyes steady as his under brows that slanted upward. Her mouth might once have had that firm line of closure, too, before it had lost too many teeth.

The father and mother could have sat for a painting, "Backwoods Pair."

But now Sojer's father was asking, "Ain't it time you make ready for them estercises, son?"

At Tolly's side, Sojer stiffened as if to meet a blow. "I got bad news last night, sir," he said in a strained voice. "They call me and tell me I — I ain't graduating."

Tolly did not want to look at the two people before her, but she could not drag her eyes away. For a moment both were held in an empty stillness. Then the father's voice rasped out.

"You mean another year befo' you gits started in that Medicinal College? Look yere, boy, I done tek about all I kin —"

Sojer answered grimly. "It ain't another year, sir. It ain't never. I'm washed up."

The ensuing stillness was more absolute, like something stretched taut between them. Tolly could hear voices bursting out of the background of indefinite sound that surrounded them before the father's came snarling into the foreground.

"You means all them years done gone for nothing? All them years of foolishment, books, books, books? Whilst yo' pa and ma work they fingers to the bone to raise ten head of chillen, and you stickin' what yo' earnt into the savings bank? And yo' ma ever sidin' with you —" He darted a malevolent glance at her and mimicked harshly, " 'Jes' yo' wait twell he a big doctor, makin' big money!' Well, I wait!"

The mother did not defend herself. She seemed hardly aware of the bitter hail of words. For a moment she lifted dim eyes to her son and quavered, "Son, never yo' mind. Ma kin hold out, long as you need her. Yo' kin go on —"

Sojer hung his head. "It's no good, Ma. I just ain't got what it takes."

The mother wiped away a trickle of tears with the back of her hand. When Sojer would not meet her imploring gaze, her hands went up to cover her contorted face, and she rocked to and fro as if in pain too great to endure.

That was only for a minute. She folded her hands in her lap, while a heavy breath hissed through her mouth, twisted out of control. Then she lifted her eyes to her son again, with an attempt at a smile.

The chiming of a chapel bell gave Tolly release from the tension. "Will you excuse me, Mrs. Pratt? I'll hardly have time to dress. — Oh, my father and mother would be pleased if you would have dinner with them after the exercises. All three of you."

The father started to speak, his lips again lifting in a snarl, but the mother raised a warning hand toward him without looking his way. She doesn't dispute him in most things, Tolly thought, but she can when there's need.

Mrs. Pratt spoke huskily but with quiet dignity. "Please to thank yo' folks, Miss — Miss Tolly. But we best be gettin' on home. It's a fur piece and our old truck lose a lot of time —"

"What about you, Sojer?" Tolly forced herself to ask.

He shrugged. "I go along with them. Where I belong."

Tolly clasped Mrs. Pratt's hand, her heart for a moment empty of everything but pity. The mother's wet eyes searched the young face before her. Their solemnity seemed to say that she did not find there all she had hoped.

"And good-by, sir," Tolly said uncomfortably, putting out her hand to Mr. Pratt, who held it limply, scanning her with savage disapproval, as if she were the cause of all their trouble.

In spite of herself, Tolly turned back to the mother. "I hope you had a good breakfast," she said awkwardly.

It was Mr. Pratt who answered, spitting out the words as if they burned his mouth. "Sho' nuff. We et like rich folks. Col' bile' yams, what we fotch from home."

Tolly gave an unhappy cry. "Oh, Sojer! You must take them to the dining room. A good hot breakfast — grits and bacon and coffee — Sojer, did you have any yourself?"

"Ain' hungry. But I take them, Tolly. And when you all done graduate and full of honors — I be gone. No more worry to you. — Please to wait whilst I take Miss Tolly to the door," he said to his parents, and walked across the big room with her.

Miss Tolly.

They paused inside the big door, and Tolly impulsively put out her hand, her lips trembling. Slowly Sojer took the hand, soft and smooth against a palm almost as hard and rough as his mother's. He looked down at the tapering brown fingers.

"I wonder," he said slowly, "I wonder do I ever see you again. Like they say, it was grand while it lasted."

"Why, Sojer, what a crazy idea! Mind you write to me. Mind you write real quick," she scolded, stretching a little higher, to set the lightest of kisses on his cheek.

Sojer put up a hand and covered the place where her lips had rested. He held it there in a gesture she would long remember. "Yes, I sho' wonder," he repeated.

Turning and fleeing blindly through the door and down the steps, Tolly also wondered.

3

For a few yards, mercifully without meeting anyone, Tolly plunged ahead, blinking the tears from her eyes and giving free course to the storm within her. Only this morning her world had looked like a glorious sunrise. In an hour it had gone flat and gray. She slackened her pace, clenching her fists till the nails bit the palms. She must not let anyone see that she was disturbed. She must not be disturbed. She would not be downed by this calamity. Commencement Day should not be spoiled.

Tolly had always loved the great days — Christmas, Easter, birthdays. As a little girl she had guarded them with a fierce possessiveness, to keep anything from marring them. "Dear God," she remembered praying, "don't let Aunt Phil die till after Christmas. Please let us have Christmas all happy."

No, Sojer should not spoil her day of triumph. She would begin by relishing this bright morning, with no cloud at all hiding its sun. She would smooth her hair, enjoying its smart new styling. She would add the merest touch of rouge to her smooth cheeks ("brown satin angel") and accent the generous curves of her mouth with lipstick. Finally, she would march in the procession like a young queen. ("Tolly baby, you sho' step out like a princess. Those feet don't hardly touch the ground.") Why must she hear Sojer's deep voice at every turn? Sojer, who had cheated at exams and hadn't been clever enough to get away with it. Sojer, for whom she had missed girl fun that could never be retrieved.

Angrily she shook back heavy hair as she swept into the dormitory and pelted up the long stair. It was framed in glass, so that she could see the campus as she went, and be seen by it.

"My land!" her roommate scolded as she burst into their room. "I began to think you were going to miss your own commencement. What ever kept you so long?"

"Oh, stuff and things," Tolly snapped. "Tell you later." She was skinning her dress off over her head. Like a whirlwind she pulled on a filmy white one, kicked off her shoes, stood on one foot and then the other to pull on the new ones. "Lucky I dressed to the top layer," she muttered, making the brown satin cheeks bloom to rose and deepening the color in the fluent lines of her lips. While her fuming roommate waited, she scrutinized her hair, lifting a curl here, patting one there.

In a few more minutes everything was under way for this supreme hour. For a little while the darkness cleared from Tolly's mind and she could forget.

In the crowded chapel the audience settled into its seats with a final burst of soft sound. The organ prelude surged out over them. The processional followed, challenging like the beat of drums and the call of trumpets. Keeping step to the music, the graduating class started down the two aisles toward the front pews, reserved for them.

Langston Todhunter walked at Tolly's side, and managed to ask, before they left the obscurity of the lobby, "Girl, what ever has become of that big lummox of yours?" His tone was flippant, but his glance sharpened with curiosity and — was it hope? Tolly shrugged and tapped her closed lips as they passed into the chapel. Sojer's name was of course in the long printed list of graduates: Sojourner Truth Pratt. Some seniors were looking inquiringly from the list to Tolly, who pretended not to notice them.

To Tolly's flushed surprise, it was her father who rose to deliver the invocation when the seniors had all seated themselves. The name on the program was that of a member of the board of trustees. Illness may have kept him away. Father proved an impressive substitute, and his inclusion should have brimmed Tolly's cup.

After a short speech by one of the trustees came the commencement address, which gave Tolly too much time for her own thoughts.

This was her commencement, she reiterated. This was the luminous goal which had led her on through all these years. Well, few great events came out quite as expected.

Langston shoved his program over to her, after scribbling on its margin, "If you aren't going home right away, let's make it an evening. That is, if your watchdog is still out of the way. Good movie at the Bingo." He poked his pen at her for an answer, and she wrote, "Don't know what my folks have planned. Tell you later."

Though sometimes irritating, Langston was fun. He, too, came from Virginia, but not from the southern part. His mother had always prided herself on their Virginia background, and when she had named her son Langston, after the only Negro United States senator ever elected from Virginia, she probably thought that this Langston also would make his mark in politics. It did not look likely. He had slid through his courses with the least possible effort, and only made an amused grimace and a jaunty answer when urged to extend himself.

"For what? You can find Ph.D.'s making up beds on the Pullmans. Me, I can easy sing the money into my pockets without all that bother. And my old man rakes in plenty from real estate and insurance. I can always get a job in his office."

Her graduation day, and it should have been Sojer's. But she was keeping Sojer strictly out of her thoughts.

The alumni honors were announced, and then the academic honors. Tolly sat straighter. Nothing could dim this shining moment. Three seniors had been initiated into Phi Beta Kappa. In dignity and a voluminous robe the registrar rose to announced their names: "Miss Bernadine Colette Adams. Mr. Benjamin Isaiah Wills. Miss Jane Emmeline Tolliver."

Nor was that all. "*Summa cum laude*, Mr. Benjamin Isaiah Wills. *Magna cum laude* —" Tolly's heartbeats shook her body so that the program on her lap set up a rustling — "Miss Jane Emmeline Tolliver."

Tolly's ears roared in the applause that followed, and she did not listen to the names of the plain *cum laudes*.

Sojer had been proud and happy over her awards. Her roommate had been enviously petulant, and Langston had depreciated their importance by the mocking effusiveness of his congratulations. In Sojer there had been no shadow of withholding. He was as selflessly glad as were her father and mother.

Yet how could he have risked ruining everything? For himself, yes, but for her, too. All the things he had said about not letting anything harmful come near her — Anger surged up in her again. He should have had better sense. After the endless hours she had wasted on him — After she had stooped to his lower status —

His face came into her mind as she had seen it that morning when he had said that maybe the crime was in being caught. His expression had been questioning, different from any she had seen before when he looked at her.

His mother's look had questioned, too. Almost as if they weighed her and found her wanting. That was a ridiculous idea.

"What makes you so nervous, girl? And kind of pale?" Langston was whispering to her. He, too, was gazing at her, but his was a probing gaze, sharp with curiosity.

"Headache," she said, and noticed that it was true.

She was relieved when President Wright came forward

to present the candidates for degrees, setting in motion the main part of the day's program. Majors in Art, in Biology, in English, which was Tolly's field, and all the rest. The time came when Tolly was climbing the platform steps on the left, receiving the book-shaped diploma, with an approving smile from the president because of her honors. She moved her tassel to the other side of her mortarboard and floated over the platform to the right-hand steps and up the aisle to her seat again.

Jane Emmeline Tolliver, Bachelor of Arts.

The Hallelujah Chorus from *The Messiah* was a fitting climax. Former members of the University Choir were invited to come forward and join with the singers. Tolly, in her cap and gown, squeezed past the other seniors in her row and went to the front with a few of the graduates. Sojer would have been among them. He had a powerful bass —

Yet the triumphant music, resounding through the crowded chapel, lifted Tolly as it always did; as it lifted Sojer. Again her eyes flooded with tears and she felt sick. For twenty years Sojer had bent every nerve to reach this point, and then — And then the madness of endangering it all, and because of her, Tolly, at least in part —

The benediction. The recessional. Family and friends surging around her, shaking hands, kissing — Forgetting for a little while —

But Langston wouldn't let her forget. "Now give,

girl," he demanded. "What's with the faithful follower?"

And as if they had been listening for the word, others of the graduates were crowding round her, some with blank wonder and alarm, some with a cat gleam in their eyes, all demanding the explanation.

"There was a mistake about his grades," Tolly improvised. How could it have been more truly a tragic mistake? — "They didn't find it out till last night. No, not this year —"

"My land, what a jolt — to you both —"

"I call it a crying shame. Couldn't they have made an exception for such a grand guy?"

"No, no, that would jeopardize all of us —"

It was not until she had escaped to the guest cottage, with her whole family around her, that the true story came pouring out. Each reacted in his own way.

"Tk, tk, tk." Sadly her father took off his spectacles and whirled them violently. "I would have banked on that lad's honor."

"I'm deeply sorry for his mother," said Mrs. Tolliver. "But I always told you, Tolly—"

"Oh, no!" Ellen exploded with a burst of tears, and went burrowing into her father's arms.

"Well, hully gee," Dabney contributed, "who ever would have thought he'd have the guts to try it?"

"Not guts, son," his father reproved. "Wrong-minded recklessness."

Sniffing and wiping her eyes, Ellen emerged long enough to whimper, "You can be darn sure it was because he was afraid of losing Tolly. If ever a boy worshiped a girl, Jane Emmeline Tolliver — Oh, it's too dreadful —"

At that Tolly's long-pent tears had their way. "It was such a wild thing to do," she sobbed after a while. "If he'd failed — honestly — he could have come back next year. But now —"

She was so sick and shaken that her mother exchanged glances with her father, and said, "Well, since there's nothing we can do for the poor, misguided boy, we'd better be arranging to settle you here for your summer courses, Jane."

"I'm not going to take a summer course," Tolly declared. "I'm — I'm going home to St. Helena with you and rest and — and pleasure myself for a change."

"But all your great plans, daughter!" her father remonstrated in a shocked voice. "All the grand things you were going to do for our people!"

"Where does it get me, this business of helping folks?" Tolly sniffed back fresh tears. "Tears me to pieces, that's all. You think I don't care what's happened to Sojer, Ellen. I care too much."

She raised her hand as in solemn vow. "Listen, every one of you. From here on out Jane Emmeline Tolliver is not involving herself with other people's troubles. No more involvements for me. And that is that."

4

Since the Tollivers decided to wait till morning and get an early start on the drive back to South Carolina, Tolly spent the evening "pleasuring herself," as she had declared she would do from now on.

Langston Todhunter was a willing assistant. His parents had gone home, but Langston had his own car and could take his time. The two of them ate at the Bingo snack bar and went to the movie, and then danced awhile in the Student Union. There they saw Ellen, dancing with one of the medical students at Meharry, across from the campus.

"Hey, what's with my cousin Orbert?" Langston accosted her with mock indignation. "Thought you were going steady."

"But he had to go on home, like most all the rest," Ellen explained with a mournful droop of her eyes and then a roguish glance at her escort.

The stroll across the campus with Langston was pleasant. It was moonlight, and the June air was languorously sweet with roses and lilies.

"You're a fun person, Lang, you really are," Tolly

said, as they lingered where the rose fragrance was dreamiest.

"Then why not go on having fun?" Langston slipped an arm round her waist. "The old man thinks you're the berries. He'd fork over the cash for a real hunk of ice for your little pinky. Why not have a spot of fun while we're young — and before the Bomb gets us?"

"Oh-oh, this is so sudden. No, I've got to look around a little before I settle down, Lang. But thank you, all the same." When he drew her closer she wriggled free. "Got to get in," she said breathlessly. "Early start to-morrow."

"Gosh, I hoped maybe the way was a little clearer now. I'm going to write to you, though. And mind you write to me. Address just Frogmore, St. Helena, like always?"

"Box 19." Tolly hurried a little, to gain the doorway of the guest house. "Night, Lang, and thank you for a pleasant evening."

"Could have been pleasanter," he reproached her.

Leaving the campus in the early morning stillness was unexpectedly sad. Surely Sojer would come striding across the deep grass before the Tolliver car carried Tolly away.

Since she was silent, her father talked more than he usually did when driving.

"Look, Papa," Mrs. Tolliver said after a while. "If you want to chatter, why don't you let Tolly drive for a spell?"

They think that will take my mind off Sojer, Tolly

thought when her father, smiling faintly, slid over to let her go round and get behind the wheel. But it would take more than that, she was sure.

Hunger was a little more successful in keeping Sojer out of her mind. They had left the campus too early for breakfast, and good restaurants open to "colored" were few. It was nine-thirty when they came to one which they knew was endurable.

"Seems to me," Dabney observed, looking with some distaste at his plate of fatback and grits, "one of the nicest things about being white would be going wherever you wanted to for meals. Mmmm, wouldn't that be something?"

"You should be thankful," his mother admonished him, "that now everyone but you can drive and we can take turns and get home as quick as we do."

"Seems like there's always something I've got to be thankful for," Dabney grumbled. "Know something?" His tone took on an edge. "Since I was ten years old I've prayed every single day that God would make me white. I sure don't call this much of an answer." He spread out his thin dark hands and regarded them angrily.

An astonished silence greeted his declaration.

"Well?" he challenged them.

"Whose son would you have been then?" his father asked.

Dabney's mouth popped open, but no words came out. He nuzzled in under his father's arm and was silent.

While food made Tolly's stomach more comfortable,

it had little effect on her mind. Where would the Pratts be eating, and what? She could see Sojer sitting in the back of the pickup truck, long fingers clasped round knees while he gazed back to where he had left her. Even when he was not smiling his brilliant smile, he never had his father's belligerent look, but a melancholy thoughtfulness. Unlike Langston's eyes, which were shallow pools that mirrored the nearest bright or dark, Sojer's were deep and profoundly sad.

He would be almost glad when the old car hiccupped and stopped and he had to search for the trouble and repair it, or when there was a flat and he had to jack up the wheel and patch it. Anything would be better than his thoughts.

Tolly was surprised to have the flow of Papa's talk interrupted by a sniffle and a gasping sob, and even more astonished to realize they came from her own self.

"Oh, Tolly, for heaven's sake!" her mother scolded. "Can't you see that you're well out of this? There must be a lack of principle in the fellow — a lowness —"

"He is not low. And I wish you wouldn't call him a fellow."

"Awfully nice people yield to temptation," Ellen reminded her mother reproachfully.

" 'They that stand high have many blasts to shake them,' " Mr. Tolliver quoted, soberly but with a flourish.

Tolly completed the quotation with a wail. "And it goes on, 'And when they fall, they dash themselves in pieces.' "

30

"Looks like you could give him a hand up again," Dabney's shrill little-boy voice put in. "I shouldn't think you'd ought to act as if you're so perfect yourself. Doesn't the Bible say not to throw a stone if you're not perfect?"

" 'He that is without sin among you, let him cast the first stone,' " Papa quoted, solemnly nodding his agreement.

"Who said I wouldn't help him?" Tolly's voice trembled. "Up to a point. I will answer his letters. But how could things ever be the same again? How could I ever t-t-trust him?" Though she was dripping tears, her sniff was angry. "I meant it when I said I wasn't going to get involved again. I'll work at something worth while, naturally, but I refuse to enter into other people's troubles. There's no percentage in it."

Her father was humming softly, as he often did when about to say something his family would not like. Tolly darted a suspicious glance at him, and he twinkled at her benignly through the gold-rimmed spectacles he still wore, unmoved by changing styles.

"I've just been thinking of a book I'm reading," he said. "By an Anglican minister. One sentence clings in my memory. The gist of it is that the Christian's worst sin is the failure to love, the refusal to commit ourselves, and the dislike of being involved. The man seems to think you can't accomplish much without doing all three."

"Ve-ry time-ly." Tolly's voice was an icicle.

31

"Daughter, I was considering it as a theme for a sermon."

"And you'd preach it straight at me. Papa, I warn you I don't like being preached at. And it won't do a speck of good."

"Maybe you have been consorting too much with those white students they have at Fisk." Papa's remonstrance was mild. "Well brought up children of our race don't sass their elders."

"Oh, they're getting up to date in that, too," Tolly snapped.

Hastily Mrs. Tolliver intervened. "Tolly, did we tell you how badly Aunt Emmeline is failing?"

"Hasn't she been failing ever since I was born?" Tolly mumbled ungraciously, declining to be diverted. "Oh, I'm sorry. You know very well how I love Aunt Emmeline. Is she down in bed?"

"Aunt Emmeline won't take to her bed as long as she can drag herself out of it."

"I'll go see her first thing. I can take her a box of candy Langston Todhunter brought me."

By rotating drivers they were able to keep going at a steady speed, always just under the miles per hour posted on the highways. Mama was always ready to give up the wheel to the next person, and the next person was always in a hurry to take over from Ellen, whose style was erratic. But it was fine to keep on all night.

"That way we save the cost of these fine motels," Papa

said with a dead-pan face, since everyone knew that those fine motels would not let them in, no matter how tired they might be.

During the day they played some of the motoring games of the girls' childhood, for Dabney's sake, and counted state licenses and the number of white cows. And when they were not playing, and Papa was not gently orating, they sang "Alouette" and "Frère Jacques" and other rounds and songs the girls had learned at school.

So the night and two days of riding passed without dragging too badly. Yet it was a delight to reach Beaufort, South Carolina, again, and the great, soaring bridge that led across to St. Helena Island.

"We used to come in by steamer," Mr. Tolliver said, as they flew across the great structure, on whose sidewalks many fishermen tried their luck. "Makes it seem mighty close to the world, this bridge. The principals at Old Penn hoped it would never come. They thought St. Helena was better off without the world. And look how they've cut out the grand old trees on Lady's," he mourned. Lady's Island had to be traversed before another bridge led them to St. Helena itself.

"Too many kids were getting run down by cars," Dabney said matter-of-factly. "Had to make it so drivers could see."

"Yes, most progress is a mixture of good and bad. Like the public school coming to St. Helena with its grand big

33

buildings. Drove out all the rickety old shack schools. But drove out Old Penn, too."

They were approaching a misty tunnel of highway, with a blacktop floor and walls and vaulted ceiling of mighty live oaks, festooned with streamers of gray Spanish moss. Ahead of them a brick church and its graveyard came into view on one side, and on the other an irregular cluster of large buildings.

"Old Penn," Ellen mused, gazing toward them. "I'm glad I could have a few grades there."

"Yes," agreed Papa, who had gone all the way through the school. "Nothing quite like Old Penn. It was a big family, with the principals our parents and the teachers our sisters and brothers. But the Community Center is doing a fine job now, and those up-and-coming young people the Friends have put there. They are helping the islanders with their problems much as Old Penn did since just after the War Between the States, when our people here were like helpless children. And they're helping us make friends with the white folks, too."

Tolly looked back wistfully. "I'm glad I had some of the grades there, too. You have fine equipment, Mama," — Mama taught at the new school — "but not nearly all the teachers are what you could call superior."

"More every year," her mother defended it.

"It takes time to get a really adequate staff, when so few of our people are educated," Papa offered. "The ones who have degrees can get better salaries elsewhere."

"And the white folks can't see that it's their own do-ings," Tolly stormed. "They won't believe it. Students with good minds — and big dreams — held back by their poor educational beginnings. It makes me furious."

Her father, driving at the time, spoke straight ahead of him. "Chinese proverb says, 'Better to light one can-dle than to curse the darkness.'"

Tolly snorted. "What earthly good is a candle? I don't propose to stumble along lighting candles and burning my fingers. Besides, have you ever tried carrying a candle on a breezy night?"

"Might be it would take torches, we've got so much dark outdoors to light." Papa's tone was thoughtful. "What did they call the kind your grandma left to you, Mama?"

"A flambeau."

Tolly had always seen it among the curios on a book-case in their living room. Its finely shaped brass handle was also a container for oil and for multiple fat wicks that fed on the oil.

"Grandma used to say they made a picture, men strid-ing through the night with the flames streaming out in the wind," Mama remembered.

"Torches in the wind," said Papa.

"Well, I'm going to let people carry their own lights," Tolly grumbled.

"But Aunt Emmeline," Dabney interrupted indig-nantly as if recalling yesterday's conversation. "Seems like you could be nice to Aunt Emmeline."

"Oh, hush, you little squirt. Who's talking about Aunt Emmeline?"

By that time they were turning in at the home driveway. They had passed small houses, prefabs which the islanders called "shell houses," and which had taken the place of the many that had been destroyed by the last big hurricane, Gracie. They had passed also a number of more substantial little dwellings in the current style. The Tolliver house was different. Though only a story and a half, it was well built in an older fashion, and stood, glossy with paint, in a yard gay with flowers. It was Tolly's birthplace, and her heart swelled with affection as she ran up its steps to the broad porch.

"I declare, I'm like a snail getting back to its shell," she laughingly scolded herself.

Mrs. Tolliver bustled around, opening windows to air out the smell of dampness, while Mr. Tolliver and Dabney brought in the girls' bags and bundles and suitcases, and Tolly's trunk.

Fondly Tolly surveyed the rooms. They were not so artistic, maybe, as the president's and librarian's at Fisk, but Tolly loved the wood paneling that Papa had put in, as darkly glowing as at the Fisk library, and the welcoming comfort of furniture and curtains.

"You prefer to have us carry your trunk to the jump-up, daughter?" Mr. Tolliver was breathing hard from his trips up and down. "Or do you desire to unpack it here and have it stored in the barn?"

Papa still called the second floor the jump-up, as the other islanders did their smaller half-stories, and for him the barn would always be the barn.

"Might as well unpack it down here and store it in the garage. And thank you kindly, Papa."

"Thank me, too," Dabney grumbled. "I been hauling your junk up for you like you was the Queen of England. Mama, I'm starving. When do we eat?"

The evening meal was quickly prepared. Mrs. Tolliver took from the freezer a kettle of Mr. Tolliver's favorite Hopping John. Pork chops were soon sizzling on the stove, giving out their own delicious savor and promising happy combination with the rice and black-eyed peas of the Hopping John. Ellen brought in lettuce and onions and tomatoes from the garden and washed and dried them for Mama, who had a skillful hand with salad dressings. Ice cream from the freezer would finish off the feast.

All bowed their heads when Papa said with deep feeling, "Dear Lord, we thank thee for our good home and our good food. We thank thee for this our corner where we can be at peace."

"No 'White Only' signs," Ellen added, when they had joined in the Amen.

"No 'Greasy Spoon' colored restaurants," Dabney put in.

After trips away from St. Helena they were especially conscious of these things since few of its seven thousand inhabitants were white.

Supper eaten, they did nothing more but wash up the dishes before climbing the stairs to their rooms and their needed rest.

The sisters' bedroom was a home product, but Mama had given rein to her inventiveness and made a virtue of necessity. The dormer windows were charming, like a storybook, curtained in sheer white dotted Swiss, and the double bed wore a Swiss flounce below the quaintest of patchwork spreads. The walls were the sunny yellow of Tolly's choice, but the next painting would give them Ellen's favorite peach-pink.

Tolly knelt on the floor a little while, looking out through leafy branches and smelling the roses that here also were in full bloom. Fireflies glimmered in the soft dark, and a mockingbird roused from its sleep to sing a sudden aria.

Where was Sojer tonight? She shuddered at the memory of cabins she had sometimes passed in southern Virginia. It would never have done, anyway, she told herself, even if he had been as fine as she had thought him. Their backgrounds were too different. In spite of all her defenses the meeting with his parents had been a shock. It was always a shock and a burden to see the underprivileged of her own people. Not that there wasn't as wide a gap between the poor whites — uneducated, undernourished, unwashed — and the upper class of whites. But the white folks seemed to ignore the fact. Many of them judged all Negroes by those who had never had a chance.

Behind Tolly, Ellen yawned deeply. Tolly looked round to see her stretched on the far side of the bed, in her frilly nightgown, her dimpled arms thrown above her head and her eyes swimming with sleep. "Aren't you ever coming, Sis?" she asked.

"In two shakes," Tolly agreed. She clicked off the electric light and lay down. "Baby doll," she said, "I sure like being in our own room, with no one but my little sis. This bed has just the right hollows in it, too. Feel good to you?" When Ellen did not answer, Tolly turned over and kissed her soft cheek, sweet from the scrubbing she had just given it.

"Mmmm," Ellen murmured, making a sleepy kiss sound which changed into the gentle cadence of sleep.

Tolly settled herself for a sleepless night, with all her thoughts bent on the reversal of her hopes and plans. Who would have supposed that two days could change things so? Change a person, too. She was not the same Tolly who had thought she could go out and help lead her people in this difficult adjustment of integration, she and Sojer working as a team. She was wiser now, she thought. Probably she could do even more good if she kept herself entirely objective, as she was determined to do.

She could not hold that position with Aunt Emmeline. Aunt Emmeline had always considered the Tolliver children her own "grands," especially since she had none left of her kin. And Aunt Emmeline is a purely sweet somebody, Tolly thought to herself, whimsically lapsing

39

into the common speech of the islanders. Aunt Emmeline would love that box of chocolates, but she must find
her some other gift, besides —

5

TOLLY was wakened by the song of early birds in the trees and the crowing of a cock in the chicken run. For a moment she lay with her eyes too gritty with sleep to be pulled open, and tried to think what a rooster was doing on Fisk campus. Then the good smells of sidemeat and frying grits ascended the narrow stair and jerked her into wakefulness. She stepped into robe and slippers and galloped down to give her mother a resounding kiss and to sniff enjoyably at the breakfast.

"Cornbread, too?" she asked hopefully, and opened the oven door a crack to answer her own question. "I'll bathe later, Mama. I'll run up and give myself a cat-wash now, and be dressed in time to set the table."

"And what may be the plan of procedure for today?" Mr. Tolliver asked a half-hour later, as the family sat happily relaxed at the end of a savory meal.

"Soon as the morning chores are done, I go to see Aunt Emmeline," Tolly said promptly. "You aiming to go over that way on any sick calls, Papa?"

Regretfully her father shook his head as he took a last swallow of fragrant coffee. "Sorry, daughter, but my pastoral duties take me today to the far side of the island. Why not give Dr. Lincoln a ring and ask if he has calls that way?"

"Uncle Doctor! Yes, and then I can walk home." Tolly excused herself to go to the telephone.

The doctor would be setting out about nine, he said, and would be delighted to have "little Jane" for a companion. So she hastened to make beds while Ellen dried dishes. Tolly's clothes were rumpled from packing, but a print that had hung all winter in her closet was clean and had retained a trace of its crispness. Here it was not dust that caused extra washing, unless there was a severe windstorm; it was dampness. Instead of a door the closet had a curtain, with plenty of space at top and bottom for the necessary ventilation. Through the bottom opening Tolly could see some of her old shoes lined up on the floor, all badly mildewed. She pulled out a pair of sturdy oxfords, rubbed them briskly, and put them on over clean white anklets.

Gifts in hand, she raced downstairs, bade her mother good-by, and hurried to the doctor's house, a five-minute walk away.

Slightly larger and more substantial than the Tollivers', the doctor's house had two full stories and shady verandas. "On the dot!" Dr. Lincoln called to her as she dashed up the steps. And Mrs. Lincoln's soft voice added, "Good to see you coming back to us. I thought you were staying for summer school."

Tolly murmured something about feeling more like

a summer on St. Helena. She was sure to be sidestepping questions till the last person on St. Helena had the explanation.

When she was on the front seat of the Chevy beside the doctor and they were spinning along the road he turned his head just enough to study her over the tops of his glasses.

"Looking poorly, Jane Emmeline. For you. You been studying too hard?"

"Not exactly." Tolly tried not to look at him, but it was no use. "Oh, Uncle Doctor," she burst out, after a few minutes of silence, "ever since I was a child for real, you've said, 'Stick out your tongue, Jane Emmeline,' and I've stuck it out. Or you'd say, 'Jemmeline, have you been shinnying up that apple tree and stuffing yourself with green apples again?' and I'd break down and admit it. You've got me conditioned." She paused and swallowed. "I've had a heavy disappointment, that's all."

" 'E disappint.' " The doctor thoughtfully quoted the older islanders. "When a beautiful girl-child is disappointed, I've learned to look for a boy-child. We men so often disappoint our women. So I don't say *cherchez la femme*, but the other way round. Surely not that fellow you introduced to me the time I visited you at Fisk? Let's see: was he named Harriet Tubman? Oh, no, it was another of our heroic women, wasn't it?"

Tolly barely smiled at the idea of Sojer as Harriet Tubman. "Sojourner Truth. Yes."

"Now I'd have banked on that boy. Premed, wasn't

he?" Frowning, the doctor deftly steered the car away from a small boy driving a cow and a donkey down the middle of the road. "I'd have thought he'd cut off his right hand sooner than disappoint the princess. Or maybe you were disappointed in his manners. Couldn't take a polish, perhaps. Though I must say I haven't noticed many manners among the pampered pets of today."

"It wasn't anything like that. Sojer was learning manners pretty well. — Oh, doctor, it was much worse; it was plain, downright dishonesty. Stupidity, besides."

Dr. Lincoln seemed intent on the road, though it was empty for a half-mile ahead. "Tk, tk, tk," he mourned, shaking his big head, "mighty hard fuh belieb that boy not hones'. Patch o' wool in the palm of his hand, Jemmeline? Oonuh certain fuh sho'?"

Tolly knew he was trying to lighten the moment by using the dialect, but she did not smile. "Oh, nothing like that. He — he cheated in exams. And he didn't have enough sense to make it look reasonable," she rushed on. "His papers were so near perfect that the high muckamucks investigated —"

Dr. Lincoln continued to study the empty road. "The unpardonable sin: to get caught. What excuse did he give for that?"

Tolly felt angrily uncomfortable, as she had on the same score with Sojer and his mother. "Oh, that he knew he couldn't pass the exams, and couldn't face the possibility of giving up his dreams."

"Such as?"

44

"You know—being a good doctor for his people. His profs said he had everything — except the preliminary education. And he could do anything with his hands. And he had a feel for diagnosis. Oh, Uncle Doctor!" She dabbed at her eyes. "He thought you were tops. Used to wonder if you'd let him work with you awhile, you being island folks and knowing them so well. And then maybe —"

"And then maybe taking over my practice when the rheumatism got too bad," Dr. Lincoln growled, his grin a twisted one, for his crippling arthritis was no joke. "And his other excuse was doubtless named Jane Emmeline, Tolly for short." He sighed heavily. "Had him going and coming, didn't it? Probably thought the end justified the means. A heap of fine folks have yielded to that temptation. Well, all I can say is I'm mighty sorry, Jane Emmeline. And here we are at your destination. Never any mistaking this place, is there? Last old-style cabin left on the island, I do believe. Even Hurricane Gracie knew better than to meddle with Aunt Emmeline and her castle."

"Want me to call for you in an hour or so?" he asked.

Tolly was having some difficulty with eyes and nose. She shook her head. "I'll walk home," she said huskily.

6

As the car sped away, Tolly stood with her hand on the gate, apparently surveying cabin and yard, but actually driving Sojer out of her mind and the tears out of her eyes.

The gate was shaky, and Tolly took her time to close it, replacing the slab wedged in to hold it. Yes, Aunt Emmeline must have failed, for she had always been fiercely determined to keep her beloved house and lot shipshape.

The yard was of clean-swept earth, patterned with the print of hens' feet, like a strange writing, and brightened by small patches of flowers. Always, Tolly thought, you could find marigolds in bloom here, orange, yellow and brown, and always a few butterflies to match them. A huge old live oak tree towered high above its roof, which sloped in a lovely line from ridge to front edge of the porch. Those protecting limbs made it look as small as a doll's house, standing there well above the ground on brick supports, itself neatly whitewashed and trimmed in the old-time blue.

The older island houses all had these little stilts, even

the large ones. Built so, they were cooler in summer, though chillier in winter.

And now Aunt Emmeline stood in the doorway, holding herself upright by a steadying hand on the door frame, while she peered at Tolly from under a protecting palm.

"Come in, come in and rest yo'self," she called tremulously. "Can't clearly make out who you be, but you welcome."

"Oh, Aunt Emmeline!" Tolly cried, running up the path. "It's me, Jane Emmeline, just home from Fisk."

"Now the good Lawd be praised!" Aunt Emmeline exclaimed as Tolly's strong young arms encircled her. "That all I need! I just tidying my house," she apologized. "Powerful slow these days. Efn you pull the chairs out on the gallery, we can sit and talk, honey chile."

Tolly's eyes filled with fresh tears as she placed the rocker, with its patchwork cushion, and beside it the stool which had been Tolly's since she was a baby, close, because of Aunt Emmeline's failing sight. Yes, Aunt Emmeline had lost ground since she saw her at Christmas time.

Leaning up against a white-aproned knee, Tolly took an old hand into her young, strong one and looked lovingly up into the old face.

Aunt Emmeline laid the other hand on the girl's head. "I so t'ankful to see my grand once mo'. I tell the good Lawd, 'Massa Jesus, old Emmeline ready fo' them golden

47

streets any time You calls her. But please, dear Massa, efn it all the same with You, let me see that sweet gal-chile once mo'.'"

She bent to study Tolly's face more closely. "Honey, you been spendin' too many night hours over them books? Cheeks use' to look like wild berries stain 'em. Not now."

Tolly bent her head over the palm, so clean and so hard; turned it and noted anew the horny nails and the dark, prominent veins.

"Yo' weepin'! Tell Aunt Emmeline what trouble you."

Tolly took a quick breath. "Oh, Aunt Emmeline! You know last summer I told you about Sojer — Sojourner Truth Pratt — and showed you his picture —"

Tolly could feel her nodding.

"Oh, Aunt Emmeline —! They caught him ch-ch-cheating! They wouldn't let him graduate — After I'd worked so hard to help him —" Her head went down on the starchy apron and she was crying like a child.

For minutes they sat so, Aunt Emmeline's free hand stroking and patting. Gradually the sobs lessened and Tolly could hear the talk of the hens and then the song of a brown thrasher and finally the sibilant hum of insects. She felt for her handkerchief, dabbed at her eyes, blew her nose, and sat up. With a shamefaced smile she blinked at Aunt Emmeline.

"Such a cry-baby," she apologized.

"The good Lawd make us so we grieve fo' the sins of

them that's dear to us," Aunt Emmeline crooned. "You still care fo' him, honey chile?"

Tolly shook her head sharply, not sure whether she was indignant at the idea or at herself. "How could I trust him again? He isn't worthy, Aunt Emmeline."

"How many of us — worthy?" Aunt Emmeline mused. "The good Lawd had to die so we could go to Glory. He forgive us, honey chile, He forgive us. Is usn too good fo' forgive others?"

Tolly blew her nose again. "I think I can — forgive Sojer," she said hoarsely. "But things could never be the same. — Aunt Emmeline, let's talk of something pleasanter. Look what I brought you." She handed her the shiny, ribbon-tied box she had laid on the steps. "And this little bottle of perfume. You love roses, and this is rose perfume."

By the time Aunt Emmeline had chuckled her pleasure over the candy and sniffed the rose fragrance, and they were each nibbling a soft, sweet morsel, the talk had got safely away from the subject of Sojer.

"But Aunt Emmeline," Tolly recalled, "you mustn't talk that way about leaving us. Do you take the medicine Dr. Lincoln brings you? Do you eat the way he says you should?"

"That Doctah!" The old woman chuckled again, richly. "I tells him, 'Jim, you big doctah to most folks, but not to Aunt Emmeline. To Aunt Emmeline you little old Jim Lincoln, shinnying up my fig tree and stuffing yo' pockets with my-own figs. How you think I mind you?' "

"But he does know what is good for you," Tolly pleaded, laughing. "And St. Helena wouldn't be St. Helena without you."

The old hand patted and the old eyes smiled and the old lips blessed Tolly. "We all got to go when our time comes," Aunt Emmeline said placidly. "When you can't see no mo' and can't hear no mo', and can't hardly walk past yo' own gate, then, honey chile, look like it time to go to heaven."

Vigorously Tolly shook her head. "We'll be eyes and ears and feet for you," she promised, her eyes filling again. Aunt Emmeline's face was beautiful, she thought, every line carved by goodness, patience, love. She must try to get pictures this summer, but no snapshot could catch what she saw. She wished she could paint a portrait or make a bronze sculpture of the noble head. "Besides," Tolly said craftily, "somebody would be sure to remodel this house if you weren't here to guard it."

"I do wonder," Aunt Emmeline said, "who gwine get this traveling old folks' home when I done with it. Sho' hope they cherish it. Efn they tear it down and put up one of them shell houses —" Aunt Emmeline left the sentence unfinished.

"Remember when I used to say, 'Tell it again, Annemmeline?' " Tolly said, settling herself more comfortably. "Do tell it again. It's been years since you did."

Laughing, Aunt Emmeline tapped Tolly's cheek, but launched not unwillingly into the old story, while Tolly half listened, soothed by the well-loved voice and the quiet drama of the storytelling. As far back as the War Between the States the islanders' art of storytelling had been reported by General Higgins, commander of the famous Black Regiment.

When a tidal wave from the West Indies had laid waste the islands, Aunt Emmeline's husband had done his best to rebuild their cabin from the wreckage. Two of their children had been drowned, and their father received injuries that shortened his life. Only one daughter was left to the little home, and she and her child had both died.

Though alone, Aunt Emmeline got along very well for years, going to the praise house three evenings a week and grieving when the meetings were cut down to one. The Tollivers had always looked after her, and she was content.

But the old cabin grew more and more "ractify," as she said, until it was clear that she could not safely stay in it. Safe or not, Aunt Emmeline stayed. She would not leave her old live oak, a seedling when the great storm struck fifty years earlier, nor her fig tree with its riches of fruit.

Then the Penn School people had an inspiration. Still in use was their first building, treasured also because it was the home of the first school for Negroes in the Deep South; still in use, but rickety and raining inside whenever there was rain outside. Also, Penn had begun to offer carpentry courses, although the islanders resisted. They associated manual labor with the terrible days of slavery, and believed that only book-learning belonged to freedom.

Now the Penn principals interested the carpentry students in a new project. They tore down the old schoolhouse, took the sound timbers to Aunt Emmeline's little farm, and there built a stout new cabin, thus keeping both Aunt Emmeline and the memory of the old schoolhouse safe. It was to live on always, they said, moved to another site when one inhabitant had finished with it, a traveling old folks' home indeed.

Coming to the close of the story, Aunt Emmeline uttered her own special chuckle, this time a soft sound of wonder. "He hold the whole worl' in His hand," she said. "And He hold Aunt Emmeline likewise. Them Penn chillen help me out of my ractify house and tote me to the new one, for I was po'ly just then. And what you think? We hardly foot the new flo' when we hears a great bang and crash. We look back, and the old cabin, it just give up and lay down. But old Emmeline was safe out from under."

It was a fact that the cabin had collapsed as if it knew its work was done. Of late years Tolly had wondered whether the Penn students had not secretly pulled out some of its props at the precise moment for a dramatic finale.

"That was Old Penn," Aunt Emmeline mused; "Father and mother, teacher and doctor to St. Helena right from the end of the War Between the States. And now Old Penn gone, saving the Community House. You maybe work in the Community House, honey chile? Aunt Emmeline sho' proud efn you help Old Penn."

"I — might help there this summer," Tolly agreed reluctantly.

"Or at Mather," Aunt Emmeline pursued the subject. "Mather always like a sister to Old Penn and help the Port Royal chillen and the Low Country like Old Penn help St. Helena. Whyn't you teach at Mather, honey chile, now you got the diploma?"

"Aunt Emmeline, I don't think it's what I want to do."

Within herself she was saying that she knew it wasn't what she wanted. For one thing, Mather teachers, long an integrated faculty, did not stay aloof from their students. From the president through the staff they concerned themselves deeply with all the girls, and now with the increasing number of boys, since the school had become coeducational. And, Tolly repeated to herself for the hundredth time, she did not mean to involve herself. She would not increase Aunt Emmeline's look of mild disappointment by making her disinclination clear, but she did not want to teach at Mather.

Just then Tolly was released from saying more. The oyster factory across the island whistled for noon, and Tolly scrambled to her feet. "Aunt Emmeline, I have to walk home, and Mama will have lunch ready. Could I fix you some lunch before I go?"

"No need, honey. I got me a tater roasting in the ashes, and fresh milk the neighbor child leave when he milk my Mahaly."

So Tolly said good-by, her mouth watering at mention of the sweet potato. A luscious morsel it would be, baked tender and oozing sweetness. No wonder it was the islanders' choice for a "piece" between meals, rather than bread or cookies.

It was warm at high noon. Sweat prickled out on Tolly's forehead and trickled into her eyes. A small boy ahead of her capered along as if to keep his bare feet from blistering. It was a relief to reach the avenue of overarching trees, where there was at least a look of coolness. She passed between the Community House buildings and the church and graveyard across from them, and came to the "principals' house," with its curious walk of great circular stones. Even these spoke of Old Penn's care for her children, for the principals had given the islanders food and clothing in exchange for the hand millstones no longer used, when they were left destitute by a hurricane.

Yes, Penn had been a blessing and a power on the island, Tolly thought soberly, and it was no wonder that Aunt Emmeline remembered it with a worshipful love. The islanders had something that marked them off from other Negroes in the Deep South, in that they were landowners, the Government letting them buy small farms on the old plantations, paying for them over the years. If Penn School had not been there, many more of them would have lost those self-respecting acres, for lack of the skill and the understanding to make them pay.

And Mather, in a different situation, had given as staunch a service and almost as long. It was still giving, as Tolly well knew, for both she and Ellen had been enrolled in it after Old Penn had closed its doors.

There was another thing that made Tolly unwilling to teach there, even if she were given the chance. Not only was the faculty as deeply involved with every student as it was possible to be, but it also discouraged harsh criticism of the white people.

Tolly tossed her head indignantly. Those white folks! For generations they had left the Negro children to scramble through schools that failed to educate them. And now, when the Supreme Court had ordered that all schools be integrated, those same white folks protested that the Negro children were too inferior to study with their own.

"They make it that way," Tolly muttered under her breath. "They give most of us no chance to learn what we need to learn. Now let's see what they can do about it. It's not my problem."

7

FOR A WHILE, Mama decided, Tolly and Ellen should do nothing but rest. Later, if they wished, they might offer their services at the Community House.

Never was there such a place to rest, Tolly thought. Though the population had grown to an amazing seven thousand, so few of these were white that the islanders were not ruffled and hurt by the daily indignities they would have suffered almost anywhere else.

To be sure, St. Helena lacked many of the conveniences the sisters had grown used to. It had no places of entertainment. But most of the islanders had radio and TV, bringing them movies and news.

"Seems like yesterday," Aunt Emmeline told Tolly, "that we get our news no way but by the 'grapevine' and the drum."

Tolly thought that she could remember hearing the drum once or twice in her early childhood, when it sounded an announcement across the island. She was sure its rattling roll had made her small spine tingle. She had always liked a poem with the phrase: "the hidden drums of Yemassee."

Tolly went often to see that Aunt Emmeline was all

right, or to bring hot biscuits or chicken stew in a Mason jar, or to hunt the eggs, since the hens laid wherever they pleased. The Tollivers had tried to persuade Aunt Emmeline to make her home with them, since none of her kin were left, but she would not be persuaded.

So they took turns, Papa and Mama and now the sisters. Occasionally Dabney accompanied them, to do some boy chores, and tease the cat, and munch enjoyably on one of those richly sweet potatoes that were usually roasting on the hearth. They all found it like stepping back into the past.

Sometimes the sisters and brother accompanied Aunt Emmeline to one of the few praise houses left on the island, only a quarter-mile away. In slavery days and for long years thereafter there had been one of the crude little chapels on each plantation, and there were still some of the older people who could not walk as far as any of the seven St. Helena churches and liked to go to the nearest praise house. Those praise houses were like her, on their last legs, Aunt Emmeline said. Soon they would be gone.

Although she had an inner sense of embarrassment at their primitive simplicity, Tolly secretly enjoyed going once in a while. For the rest of the little audience the pattern of worship was normal and natural.

The first meeting night after "school-break," the three young Tollivers and Aunt Emmeline walked slowly over to the meeting through the early dark. No special hour was set. As soon as the people had done their chores they came, often not changing from their work clothes.

Keeping for a while to the road, the girls walked on each side of Aunt Emmeline, grasping her arms to steady her. Dabney cavorted ahead of them, leaping high to grab a pennon of Spanish moss or climbing into a live oak to drop acorns on them as they passed below.

When they cut across a patch of woodland they had to separate, for the path was narrow and winding. They stepped aside from it at their peril, for cockspurs as well as kadyah vine infested the uncultivated ground, grabbing and stabbing at skirts and ankles. At one point Aunt Emmeline wanted them to turn off the path, pushing aside the bushes until they came to a tiny clearing. Aunt Emmeline, with a sorry cluck of tongue, broke away some intruding branches.

"He long gone," she murmured. "So long."

The fading light shone on low graves, small and large. It was a large one that held Aunt Emmeline's gaze. Embedded in it were old medicine bottles, a cup, a plate. Staunch Christian though she was, Aunt Emmeline had felt it safer to place some of her husband's favorite possessions on his grave, as well as bottles that had held his "spoon medicine" during his last illness. With his treasures in reach, his spirit would not be tempted to come hunting for them in the cabin.

Tolly knew that there were other superstitions of her ancestors that Aunt Emmeline had not lost. She still used spells to set her jelly, bring the butter when she churned, and make her hens lay well.

Aunt Emmeline pointed to another of the longer mounds. "My last grand. None of my kinnery left on the Lawd's green earth."

Dabney managed to turn a cartwheel without touching one of the graves. "Won't we be late to praise house?" he inquired.

Returning to the path, they crossed the fields in the deepening dusk with its firefly lanterns. As they left the thicket, Tolly had pulled from a live oak a handful of the cascading gray moss, to comb the prickles from skirts and socks. "Talk about these modern lint removers," she said to Ellen, handing her a bunch of the crinkled gray fiber.

The praise house was a cabin set in the middle of a cotton patch, its one small room filled with crude benches. At the glassless windows the heavy shutters were flung wide to let in the soft air. At the front stood a small table, as crude as the benches, an open Bible, a hymnbook, and a tall kerosene lamp. Most of the benches were taken, practically all by the old and the very young, and Aunt Emmeline and her escorts half filled another one.

The leader, one of the old men of the island, had just opened the hymnal when a sound at the door made Tolly glance round. For a moment her heart stood still. The figure entering almost filled the doorway. He had to bow in order to avoid striking the lintel, and enter on the bias because his shoulders were so broad. For an instant, seeing him in the dim light, Tolly thought it was Sojer, his eyes fastened upon her.

The man's eyes were instead laughing provocatively at Ellen. Tolly looked in time to see Ellen turn back toward the leader, a smile crinkling her creamy cheek.

"It's that Stormy Waters we used to know," Ellen whispered. "Cute, isn't he?"

The leader was lining out a hymn, and the people repeated each line after him. The custom was not so necessary as a few years ago, for there were now few in the room who could not read. It was still needful in another way. There was only one hymnal, and only one lamp. The congregation could not have seen to read even if they had had books. Though still shaken by her moment's fancy, Tolly automatically lifted her rich contralto and sang.

She was scornful of herself for the joyful leap of her heart and its sick sagging. Such foolishness on her part was another argument for being objective, for keeping outside other people's dreams, hopes, troubles.

The hymn had been sung, with feet tapping in time to the music. Ellen's elbow prodded Tolly, who became aware that the leader was peering at her over the spectacles that had slid down on his nose.

"— raise a spiritual?" he was asking.

"He's asking you," Ellen whispered.

Her mind fumbling, Tolly thought of a line that Aunt

Emmeline had sung the other day. Tolly loved it, partly because of the entirely different ways in which it was sung by Aunt Emmeline and by Marian Anderson.

Folding her hands lightly in her lap, Tolly relaxed, breathed deep and began:

"He holds the whole world in His hand."

Ellen's small, true soprano joined in, and Aunt Emmeline's frail, quivering voice — distilled sweetness, Tolly had always thought it — and presently a strong tenor that must be Stormy's. It was not a spiritual often used in the praise house, but one by one the other voices came in, carried by their love of music. Soon the little place rocked with swelling sound and with the cadenced tapping of shoes on the floor.

Tolly had read what the world thought of her people's singing. Tonight she sensed its quality anew. It was release from present-day shackles and shortages. More, it was a direct communication with God.

When the room was still again, except for the restless stirring of a small child and the coughing of his elders, Unc' Nicodemus leaned over the open Bible and read. Tolly's eyes were fixed upon the strong planes of his face, eerily lighted from below, but her thoughts departed.

Perhaps the best way to get over Sojer was to find someone else. But where? She wasn't a flirt, like her adored Ellen, and she couldn't waste time on anyone like that Stormy. He had barely got through high school over in Beaufort, and was working in the oyster factory.

She could think of no unattached St. Helena man who was any more suitable. She wondered if there were men teachers at Frogmore School, if she decided to teach there.

The most likely hunting ground, she thought seriously, was probably in graduate school. Any Negro student there would have had to leap the high hurdle of his B.A. But he'd probably be married —

Evidently Unc' 'Demus had finished his discourse, for Aunt Emmeline was praying. Tolly always listened to Aunt Emmeline. Like some others of the older islanders, she spoke in untaught poetry.

"Good Massa, seems like Yo' chillen bound to go footing the bad paths. Draw us back, kind Massa. Hook Yo' rod about the neck of our spirit and draw us back. We kneel our hearts down befo' You."

Others prayed, another hymn was sung, and Unc' 'Demus pronounced the benediction. The worshipers came, eyes and smiles shining out of the dimness, and shook hands with Tolly and Ellen.

Stormy was among them. "Kin I walk you home, Sis' Ellen?" he bantered, gazing with frank admiration at her flushed prettiness. "You fetched me here. I see you coming. It only right I walk you back."

"We four are together," Ellen said demurely. "My bubbah and sis and Aunt Emmeline."

"And Stormy makes five," he said with assurance. When all the small congregation had shaken hands and gone out, he and Ellen trailed along behind Aunt Emmeline, Tolly, and Dabney.

They left Aunt Emmeline in her own cabin, after lighting the lamp for her, and walked the rest of the way by twos. Tolly maneuvered herself and Dabney to the rear, so that she could supervise and also hasten the steps of the other two. She must have a serious talk with Ellen, she thought anxiously. This Stormy was a handsome fellow, and Ellen susceptible. He could destroy all her fine prospects.

Thinking of this, when they reached home she determinedly joined the two in the porch swing. Dabney walked the railing, balancing ostentatiously and grabbing at the swing to steady himself, but his desire to pester his sister soon gave way to sleepiness.

"You-all going to watch for sun-up?" he demanded with a tremendous yawn. "Well, a good night to all three." He went in.

Soon after that, Mrs. Tolliver peered from the door. "Girls, do you know what time it is? Come get your beauty sleep," she called. Then, as if she had just caught sight of a third person, she added, "Oh, excuse me. I see you have a friend with you."

"It's Stormy Waters, Mama," Ellen said with a pout in her voice. "Surely you can see it's Stormy Waters. You've known him ever since he was born, I reckon."

"Indeed I have—" Was Mama's emphasis significant? — She came out and shook hands with Stormy, who rose to give her his place.

As Mama had plainly intended, the group dissolved and Stormy took his leave.

"Of all things!" Ellen exploded, when the girls had followed their mother into the house. "Is that the way you're going to encourage any beaus who come around?"

"If they're no more suitable than Stormy Waters," her mother said coldly.

"That's right, Ellen," her sister seconded.

8

THAT NIGHT Ellen went to bed and to sleep without kissing any of her family. Next morning she was sweet, soft, and sad, and all the Tollivers, against their better judgment, petted her.

She said, eyes wide and pitiful, "You darlings, you will let me go places with Stormy, won't you? He wants to take me over to a movie. A girl gets so lonesome." She quivered her soft chin.

Mr. Tolliver cleared his throat and spoke ponderously. "You are well aware that our children's happiness is one of our dearest desires. Let me make inquiries, daughter. A year or two ago, this young Waters was in some sort of trouble."

"As if I can't look out for myself!" Ellen wailed. "You don't seem to realize that a college girl is used to freedom. I'll simply wither up and die if I can't have any young fun."

"I will make inquiries." Her father was inflexible.

"Oh, very well!" Ellen's soft-eyed pleading froze to an icy haughtiness. "Very well, but there is no fairness in treating me like this."

"Tolly is going over to Aunt Emmeline's this morning," Mrs. Tolliver coaxed. "Why not help her carry things, Ellen?"

"Certainly, if I'm needed," Ellen consented coldly.

"Why, there's the postman," Tolly exclaimed, not knowing whether to spank her babyish sister, or kiss her, or laugh. "He's early today."

Dabney scrambled with them out to the box beside the road, and passed out their mail importantly. The girls dropped down on the grass to read it while he ran in the house with the rest.

"Easy enough to tell when you young ladies get home from college," the postman called back to them. "Can't hardly get all the letters in your box."

"I got one from Orbert," Ellen told her sister, her reproachful dignity melting.

"That flip young cousin of Lang's," Tolly said resignedly, remembering to smile and wave as the postman's car went into motion.

Ellen peered at the stack Tolly was shuffling through. "Isn't that one from Lang? And the next one — I'd know that writing anywhere. Sojer, no?"

The penmanship was stiff and the paper sleazy and gray. Tolly nodded absently.

Ellen was reading with stifled giggles. "Listen to this, Tolly: 'It's been cloudy ever since they tore you away from me, baby. Did you run off with the sun?' Isn't he a card, for true? And listen to this —"

Tolly sighed with exaggerated patience. "Did it ever

occur to you that I might want to read my own mail, baby sis?"

"Sojer's letter? Why, when you're through with him?"

"But I'm still concerned about what he's doing. Hush, lambie, till I skim through —"

Expression as well as penmanship was stiff and cramped. "Perhaps I should wait and let you write first, like that rule you told me that a boy should wait for the girl to smile and nod. But seems like I've got to write. I got a cotton-chopping job soon as we came home. Ma says I do nothing but sing the blues and snap at everybody. That's how life looks to me now, and I don't know how it will get any better. I do not blame you if you do not answer this, but I pray you will."

Tears sprang to Tolly's eyes and were dried by quick anger. Why couldn't he stand up for himself? Now if it had been Langston who had cheated — But Langston probably had cheated. If it had been Langston who was caught and disgraced — But Langston would not have been caught, or if he had been, he would have shaken off the disgrace as if it were nothing. She opened his letter.

"Hard-hearted Tolly," it began. "Have you grown any kinder in these months that we have been apart? Hey! Just took a squint at the calendar. It isn't months. It's only two days. Incredible. Wish you were here for the big party some of my pals are throwing for the conquering hero. That's me, in case you didn't know. They've hired a combo. One of the fellows has a swell big recreation room. His dad's a lawyer. Everything will be topnotch, except for the topnotch queen. She's marking time on a sleepy old island. Pretty swell gals here, though —"

"What does Langston have to say?" asked Ellen, when she had reread her own letter.

"Nothing," Tolly answered with a yawn. "And he takes five pages to say it." She stuffed the letter back into its envelope and her bundle of letters into her handbag and jumped up. "We better get going. And let me ask a favor — don't make any more inquiries about Sojer. Way I'm feeling right now, if I never hear his name again it will be too soon."

But she heard it as soon as they reached Aunt Emmeline's house. Aunt Emmeline had not outgrown her love for romance, and her eyes brightened at sight of the girls' bundle of mail.

"You hear from that Sojourner chile? He all right, honey?"

"Chopping cotton. That's about all he has to say."

"Aunt Emmeline, she is the hard-heartedest girl you ever saw. That poor boy! I had a good letter from Orbert. You remember I told you about Orbert. He's the one that sings like an angel."

"Only angelic thing about him," Tolly grumbled.

"Aunt Emmeline," Ellen went on. "You know Stormy Waters?"

"Stormy Waters," mused the old woman, her accent softening all the r's. "Sho'. He the little fellow was born

68

in the next to last big storm we have. Ain't so many gives their chillen basket names no mo', but Sally Waters, she couldn't pass up the chance. Stormy Waters. It kindly like a hymn tune. What the little fellow been doing, Ellen baby?"

Ellen snickered. "He's no little fellow. He grew up while your back was turned, Aunt Emmeline. You'd have heard, though, if he'd been mixed up in any great scandal lately. My folks think I shouldn't go anywhere with anyone who hasn't a college diploma and church membership. Aunt Em, I'm young. You tell them I'm only young once and I've got to have fun."

"That's the truth, Ellen baby," Aunt Emmeline agreed, nodding till her starchy white headcloth bobbed up and down. Hers was one of the few old headcloths, like a classic drapery, still worn on the island. "I mind well how I was raven for pleasure when I was a young small gal-chile like you."

"Well, my land!" Tolly snapped. "Who doesn't crave fun, Ellen Tolliver? You'd think I wasn't human. Or that I was twenty-nine instead of nineteen."

"But you're so cool and superior," Ellen accused. "You sort of stand on a pedestal and hold your skirts away from the masses. Me, I like people. And if I don't get a chance to have fun while I'm young — well, I just warn you, I'll do something desperate."

"The chile got a warm heart and strong feelings," Aunt Emmeline nodded.

"Believe it or not, it's because of my own warm heart

that I'm trying to keep away from folks. If I let myself, I'm hurt and hurt and hurt again. I'm just plain sick to death of suffering for folks who aren't worth it —" Tolly's voice broke and she sat sniffing and dabbing at her eyes while the rest looked uncomfortable. "But I can't keep aloof from you, baby sis, and I can't stand it to see you running with anyone so worthless."

"What if you gwine along, honey chile?" Aunt Emmeline suggested. "What they call 'em? Chapelroni? Reckon that would be because they keep the younguns safe as churches," she concluded drily.

"If Stormy could get you a date, Tolly?" Ellen asked with sudden eagerness.

"Likely Mama and Papa would consent to your going with Stormy if it was a double date," Tolly considered, drawing down her upper lip to control the sniffing. "But it would have to be somebody with a little sense. You tell Stormy that."

Aunt Emmeline was rocking slowly, her eyes fixed on distance. "They do tell that Rich Corwin, he home for vacation. You mind his mother come from up North — Hayet her name — to find her onliest kinnery, her great-grandma. And when she through Mather School and then college, she marry with Richard Corwin. He County Agent on Lady's Island these many years. Rich, they call their first boy-chile, and he smart and educated."

Tolly looked faintly interested. "I read a book about Harriet and Granny and Richard. — Well, you might suggest that Stormy ask this Rich Corwin." She was feeling a stir of expectancy. The beginning of summer had lacked something; it had lacked boys. "But I wonder what your Stormy calls a good movie, Ellen. What do you bet it's years old and we've seen it twice already?"

"Too bad they don't pleasure themselves here on the island like they use' to do," Aunt Emmeline mourned. "Play parties and reels that were purely fun. Not no mo'. Too old-fashion'."

Tolly looked thoughtful. "Why couldn't we get up an old-time party? Maybe folks would like it just because it would be such a change. And Ellen and I have been doing reels at Fisk."

"Tolly, I do believe you've got something there." Ellen spoke with a solemn ardor that made Tolly laugh.

"But now, Aunt Emmeline," she asked, "what can we do for you before we go on home? I think we'll stop by Community House and see if they have work for us."

"Mighty tasty, the soup yo' ma send me, and the cake. I don't need nothing, honey chile. But I too t'anksful you do something for Ol' Penn. And you figure any mo' about Mather?"

"Oh, that reminds me," Tolly said. "There was a letter from Mather in that pile of mail. Mind if I see what's in it?"

As the old woman nodded expectant consent, Tolly opened the letter. "Hm," she murmured as she read, "hmmmm. Now what do you know about that!"

"For goodness' sake," Ellen exploded, "what can we

71

know about it until you tell us?"

Frowning and smiling and shaking her head, Tolly thrust the typed sheet back into its envelope. "Miss Andrews is just about the nicest somebody. And sweet to ask me. But Mather is not for me."

Ellen went off like a firecracker. "Oh!" she sputtered, grabbing for the letter. "How cryptic can you get?"

"Calm down, calm down," Tolly adjured her. "It is an invitation to teach at Mather this coming year. Their teachers all have Master's degrees, but since I'm planning to go on for mine at once —"

"My little Jane Emmeline teaching at Mather," Aunt Emmeline crooned, an eloquent wetness in her eyes and in the deep furrows below them. "I give t'anks to the good Lawd my little honey chile lend a hand to Mather, when Mather been so good to usn."

"Oh, but I can't accept!" Tolly cried, her face puckering. And as Aunt Emmeline looked up in pained surprise, she dropped down beside her, clasped one of her hands, and gazed up remorsefully into her face. "I can't explain it, but I just can't, Aunt Emmeline. And don't you think I can help just as much by teaching this coming year at St. Helena School? You know they never can get enough really good teachers."

"And Tolly's really good," Ellen said a shade sharply. "All the same, sister," she went on in a changed tone, "if you're going to switch plans just like that, why shouldn't I? I'm sick to death of school. I don't reckon I'll go back to Fisk come fall."

Tolly sprang to her feet in alarm. "Don't be absurd," she stormed. "Of course you're going back!"

"Well, if you gave up your plans," Ellen said sulkily. "Weren't you set on graduate work this summer?"

"But I'm going to do graduate work as soon as I earn enough to go away," Tolly declared. "Colorado University, maybe. I may have changed my mind about some things, but I'm bound to prepare for serving our people. In the mass. The only ones I'm going to single out are Ellen Pinckney and Jane Emmeline Tolliver. So there."

9

THE PLAN for double-dating worked out, though Stormy was at first reluctant to ask Rich Corwin.

"He thinks he's the greatest," Stormy grumbled. "Since he been to college up North he got no time for St. Helena folks. And my own brother got more life to'm in a minute than Rich got in a year."

"But I'd really like to meet this Rich," Tolly coaxed, and Stormy finally agreed to ask him.

Their first meeting was a preliminary to the old-fashioned party. Ellen and Tolly had spent a whole dinner hour getting the senior Tollivers to talking about the traditional St. Helena festivities, which had still been going on when Mama married Papa and came to live on the island. Papa laughed so hard over some of their memories that his spectacles flew into the gravy.

"Mind," he said, while Ellen was carrying the gravy bowl to the kitchen and fishing out the glasses, "I was not yet a church member at the time of the adventure I just mentioned. It is only recently that church members have been allowed to dance the reels."

Rich Corwin had been studying "ancient" history with his own parents, he told them when he came that evening. Now if they only had a good place to hold their party, it would be clear sailing.

"Mmmm," Papa cogitated. "You reckon you make some money out of it? You almost have to, if you follow the old ways. Supposing you were to make it a benefit for the church — our church, for instance — I don't doubt but one of the elders would allow you to use old Fidelity schoolhouse. It's standing idle now, since St. Helena public school accommodates all the children."

So it was worked out, with cokes and other pops purchased at wholesale and to be sold to breathless dancers, and a booth for watermelon and for chitlings.

Meantime the Tolliver family were getting acquainted with Rich, and found much about him to discuss. Mama considered him practically perfection, his clothes were so neat and his manners so good. Papa liked the steady look in his eye, but wondered if the boy had laughs enough in him. Ellen said that he was a living doll, but Stormy had more life, and as for Orbert, that child could keep you in stitches at a funeral.

Rich had a little car, too, which was a decidedly attractive feature, with almost as much charm as the clear eyes which had a way of focusing so keenly on the person he was talking to that he gave the impression of mind reading. — "Got no place to hide," Dabney grumbled. "That Rich's eyes go burning into you like — like Uncle Doctor's flashlight."

On the evening set for the party, the four young people started out across the island in Rich's well-kept if ancient

75

convertible. Both boys carried guitars with them, for both were good players.

"Sho' feel like a storm," said Stormy, wiping his neck and forehead with a big bright handkerchief.

"But it's nice now. And what fun to ride in an open car," gurgled Ellen.

"Keen," Tolly agreed, throwing back her head to get the full rush of soft air, which had only a hint of evening coolness in it. Both girls had knotted scarfs around their carefully combed hair, to keep the humidity from curling it too much. "I hope people won't be so scared of storm that they won't come."

By the time they reached the school, which was on the opposite side of the island, any fears as to attendance were quieted. Cars of all kinds were gathered around the building, along with one of the little island ponies called tackies.

"Dad can remember," said Rich as he slipped the key from the ignition and dropped it into his pocket, "when they always had the big black boiling kettles in the yard, with eel stew cooking, and chitlings and maybe Hopping John."

"And I suppose the old drums rolled out the invitation," Tolly said rather wistfully. "Much more exciting than our common posters thumbtacked up in the stores."

"Hey, you!" Stormy called back to them, he and Ellen having scrambled out ahead, "Take yo' foot in yo' hand. They're waiting for us."

Beside him, Ellen was jigging with eagerness. "Hur-ry, hur-ry, hur-ry!" she cried, imitating an auctioneer. "Not much more than room for us four."

They were enthusiastically greeted when they pushed into the crowd. More accurately, their guitars were welcomed. "Two boxes!" someone yelled. "Two! We began to think we got to go all the way back to the old times, and dance by the old sticks."

"Old sticks ain't too bad at that!" As he said it, a big, grinning man beat a rousing ratatatat on the wall, the rhythm strong and marked.

"Fine and dandy," Rich commended. "You go ahead and we'll follow you." He unslung the guitar from his shoulder and leaned up against the wall beside the wielder of the stick to tune it.

The one big schoolroom had been swept earlier that day, and the benches and desks pushed against the walls, some of them forming makeshift booths where the soft drinks and boxes of crackerjack could be sold. The chitlings they had not been able to find, but a long desk was heaped with the dappled green of watermelons, one of them cut to reveal its inviting juicy redness. Sacks of grunnets or peanuts were piled on another desk.

Tolly surveyed the crowd with amused interest. The young islanders, around her own age and younger, looked a little as if they were slumming, their expressions plainly patronizing these queer old ways. The scattering of folks middle-aged and older, some of whom had been pressed into service at the booths, were grinning happily as if at the recovery of something they had lost.

But when the guitars struck into a reel tune, after several fumbling starts, all attention was turned to the music. It swerved momentarily when an old man came shuffling into the room, his toothless mouth open in a delighted grin.

At once several voices set up a pleased outcry. It was Unc' Bill, one of the oldest islanders, and moreover a famous caller of dances. He was soon established on the school platform and the fun began.

"Say, young gals, won't you come out tonight?"

Unc' Bill's voice, cracked and rusty, gradually fell into something of the old swing:

> *"Won't you come out tonight,*
> *Won't you come out tonight?*
> *Say, young gals, won't you come out tonight,*
> *And dance by the light of the moon?"*

"I didn't know till lately that the Western square dances were so much like our Southern reels," Tolly said breathlessly, as she paused at the end of a set and stood beside Rich.

"Hands around all!" yelled Unc' Bill into the chatter and rustle and shift of feet, and they all resolved themselves into a ring, irregular because of the improvised booths.

"Ladies to the center, gentlemen surround 'em!"

The circle broke into two concentric rings.

"Make a basket! Now wheel the basket!"

The double ring spun faster and faster till it broke of its own speed.

"Now right hand to yo' pahdnuhs! Do the grand right and left!"

By the time that reel was over, both Tolly and Ellen were laughing breathlessly. Others were laughing, too, eyes and teeth shining with the new-old experience.

"Fun!" Ellen cried.

"More fun than a barrel of monkeys," Tolly agreed.

By the end of another reel the room was stiflingly hot and everyone was ready to rest, not least Unc' Bill, whose face was shiny with sweat. He had been like one galvanized to active life after a long sleep, and now he was limp from the unusual effort. Rich and Stormy swung their "boxes" around to their backs, bought four cokes, and sauntered outside with the girls.

"It's so still," Tolly marveled, "and so hot! I think the weather really is working up to something, don't you?"

"All signs point that way," Rich agreed. "And Maum Hannah — that's my grandmother — says the misery in her joints is a sure sign."

The four strolled into the darkness, which seemed a shade less hot than where light and people streamed out of the schoolhouse doors. Stormy cupped a hand under

79

Ellen's elbow, and occasionally took a sip of coke and executed a pirouette at the same time.

"Isn't he the stepper?" Rich waved his coke bottle at the two ahead of them. "So plumb full of spirits he can't keep them corked."

"But no ambition. Now you're so different, Rich."

"That may be my Yankee blood — my darnyankee blood. Mother came from up North —"

"I know," she assented. "She was in a book."

"So was my dad," he said almost jealously. "I don't know just where his ambition came from. Penn School and Mother, maybe."

"But you — what are you going to do?"

"I'm studying law."

"Going to practice up North?" she asked.

Taking a deep draught of coke, he shook his head. "No," he answered when he had wiped his mouth. "Right here on these islands. We haven't got any lawyers of our own here. I don't know anything better I could do. It may take me a good while to get ready, though. Spent too much of last semester in jail. Jailbird Corwin, that's me."

"Jail?" Tolly demanded incredulously. "Oh — Freedom Rides? Sit-ins?"

"Both. Ever take part in any?"

"I'm not sure I believe in it," Tolly objected. "Don't you think education is the answer? Once every last Negro is educated — And now that we have the law on our side, oughtn't we to let it take its course?"

Their discussion was interrupted by a shriek from Ellen, who turned at that moment and stumbled back to her sister and Rich, clutching at them with frightened little hands.

"Rattlesnake!" she gasped. "Smell it? Listen. You can hear it, too."

Tolly and Rich had stopped, and now they strained eyes, ears — and noses — ahead of them in the darkness. A dry clicking was clearly audible. "And I do smell something," Tolly said.

Stormy was already in action. Plunging into the underbrush beside the road, he laid about him with a vigorous pop bottle.

"Oooh, Stormy!" squealed Ellen, "be careful!"

As if in answer Stormy stooped, swung something around his head and sent it slithering into the far bushes. Or did Tolly only imagine she saw it slithering in the darkness? Then Stormy came back and appropriated Ellen, who cooed tremulously at him.

"You're so brave!" she quavered.

But Rich laughed and slapped Stormy on the back. "Smart piece of work, kid!" he crowed, reaching into Stormy's pocket before the boy could stop him. "Look, girls! Wedge of watermelon for the smell. You can hardly tell rattlesnake odor from melon. And what did you use for the rattle, big boy?"

Sheepishly grinning in the flashlight beam Rich turned on him, Stormy drew from another pocket the dried rattles of a real snake.

"Good show!" Rich applauded, as if he really thought so.

Stormy seemed as agile of thought as of foot, and slapped his leg, guffawing. "Sho' did fool this little gal!" he said, and cupped his hand under her elbow again.

"What time is it?" Tolly held her wrist under the flashlight. "Good land, Ellen, we'd better be making haste home. — Papa can be mighty strict about when we get in," she explained to the boys.

Rich nodded. "Dad's that way about my sis."

"Just one more reel!" Ellen coaxed, seconded by whistles and calls from the schoolhouse doors.

"Where's them boxes?" the boys chanted. "Want them boxes."

"One more fast one, do you think?" Rich asked Tolly. She yielded. "Just one."

When at last they drew up before the Tolliver house, Tolly could hear the slow creak of the porch swing. Her parents were still up.

"It was fun," she told Rich as she got out. "Thank you a lot."

"But you never did tell me anything about your plans. Can I come back and find out?"

"Why, yes," Tolly agreed. "Phone first to be sure I'm not at the Community House or somewhere."

It was pleasant, she thought, as she and Ellen opened the gate and walked up the path, to have as nice a boy as Rich wanting to come again. To be sure, he wasn't so big a person as Sojer. He wasn't so big, she corrected herself, as she had believed Sojer was. She wondered whether Rich wasn't a little too sure he was right in everything he did and thought. Though in a nice way.

"Have a good time?" Mrs. Tolliver asked, fanning herself vigorously.

"Oooh," Ellen squealed, "more fun! Hadn't had so much fun in a blue moon."

"Yes, but a blue moon is about as often as I could take it," Tolly added.

"Stormy says there's a swell comedy coming next week to Beaufort," Ellen insinuated. "Rich will probably ask you, Tolly, if I can't be trusted alone with Stormy."

"Mmmm, we'll see. Any more news of the hurricane?" Tolly noted that the radio was turned toward the open window.

"There is hope that it will by-pass us this time. But at the least we shall have high winds here." Papa rose and stretched decorously. "We'll be up bright and early and see that everything is tightly secured."

10

BEFORE Tolly's sleep was half out, she was hustled awake by the rising tempest.

"We are not likely to get the force of it, though," her father said, when he came to breakfast after fastening gates and henhouse doors, and tying up the porch swing so that it should not be a battering-ram and break the window.

"I wonder how Aunt Emmeline will be?" Tolly asked anxiously. "Could we go over and look after her? Ellen is sleeping like a baby, but Dab and I —"

"I need to see to Uncle Nicodemus in this blow," her father said, eating hurriedly. "He is too feeble to meet emergencies. I might take you two and go on to his place. Come back and pick you up when I've seen to him. He's poorly, besides."

"But do look out for falling trees and things," Mrs. Tolliver fretted, knowing that it would be useless to try to keep them at home.

As soon as they got out on the road, even the Tollivers' heavy old car quivered in every inch. "Folks may laugh all they please at my antique Dodge," Mr. Tolliver said, hunching himself over the wheel, "but their new, light ones would blow right off the highway."

Great old oaks tossed their mighty boughs like grasses in a breeze; now and then a branch broke with a cannon-shot report. When they reached Aunt Emmeline's place, they found her with both arms wrapped round a porch post, evidently unable to advance or retreat. Gripping her on right hand and left, Tolly and Dabney pushed into the house with her.

"But I got to see to my po' little old fowls!" she said, as soon as she could speak. "They houses blow clean away efn we don't fix'm."

Looking out through a crack in a shutter Tolly could see the triangular coops already running crazily across the yard, and the hens, doubtless clucking their danger call, being blown as well.

"Dab and I will try — You stay here, Aunt Em —"

Looking back as they ran and were blown in great leaps across the yard, Tolly saw that Aunt Emmeline had not stayed. She stood pressed close against the cabin wall, out of the full sweep of the wind. Brother and sister raced on after the hens, grabbed them, were savagely pecked. "Dab, shove some of the coops down under the house," Tolly shrieked. "We'll try to — corral the hens under them — then go after the chicks —"

If there had been time, Tolly would have laughed at the hens, glaring out of feathers blown every which way. But she ran and seized and imprisoned, while Dabney dashed in pursuit of another coop, which rose in air repeatedly and banged down again, making long leaps like a demented goat.

With a rumpled hen under each arm, Tolly stopped and huddled against the wall beside Aunt Emmeline to get her breath.

"Po' little old fowl babies," Aunt Emmeline was moaning.

"There's a bunch of them out under the live oak, huddled flat to the ground." Looking anxiously over her shoulder Tolly dashed back under the cabin with her captives. "If only the tree doesn't blow down — there goes Dab after them — Oh, Dab!" she screamed. "Get out from under —"

For one of the large branches was torn from the tree with an eerie screech. It came crashing down just as Dabney dropped to his knees beside the little huddle of white fluff and covered his head with his arms.

"Lie flat!" Tolly shrieked.

The bough had fallen across his backward-stretched feet and pinned him tight. Tolly started toward him, but Aunt Emmeline — how, the girl could never understand — was tottering ahead of her. After one terrified upward glance the old woman flung herself forward over the trapped boy. With sick horror Tolly heard and saw another great leafy limb wrenched free, hurtling down with a rush and roar and completely covering the two prone forms.

With frantic uselessness she was tugging at the

branches, blown away from them and struggling back again, when another figure came zigzagging across from the road. It was her father. Without words he bent to the task and together they uncovered the inert bodies. No sound or motion came from Aunt Emmeline, but grunts and little yelps from Dabney, thrust flat on his face by the combined weight of the old woman and the live-oak limbs.

"Lie still, son —" His father put his mouth to the boy's ear, and Tolly could barely hear him above the tumult. "We — must get her into the cabin —"

"There's an old shutter under the house," Tolly gasped, recalling First Aid rules about moving the injured.

"No time — Got to risk it — You grab hold of her feet and I'll —"

They staggered across the yard with their burden, thankful it was no farther. Lungs fighting painfully for breath, they got the slight body into the cabin and with difficulty reversed its position.

"Now — bubbah —"

"Ow — ow — ow!" the boy cried, as they tugged away the branch that had pinned his legs. "Are my legs broken, Papa?"

"Just bruised, praise God. Way they're lying — they're probably not broken. Make a chair, daughter. We'll — get him in and find out—"

It was another fight through the storm to the cabin door, Dabney's arms clutching their necks and Dabney muttering and squealing with pain. They sat him in Aunt Emmeline's old rocker and turned to look at the bed. Aunt Emmeline's face was the color of wet clay.

"But she's breathing!" Tolly cried, dropping to her knees beside her.

"I'm bleeding to death," Dabney moaned in a dying voice. "Will they have to amputate my legs?"

His father was already examining them. "Nothing that won't heal up in a week, son. Look, I can move them up and down — nothing broken — and this gash across the calf — all right for it to bleed —"

"But like enough Aunt Emmeline has given her life for you." Tolly's voice was thick with tears. "Oh, Aunt Emmeline, speak to us!"

The wrinkled tissue of lids quivered and lifted enough to show a line of yellow-white eyeball. The purplish lips moved. "He all right? The baby boy?"

"Oh, Aunt Em!" Tolly sobbed. "Dab's okay. Only scratched."

"Scratched!" Dabney piped indignantly. "Baby boy!" He had been left alone as Mr. Tolliver joined Tolly and stood looking down anxiously at the frail figure on the bed.

"I must locate the doctor." Mr. Tolliver's voice was troubled. "You think some of that tea — real strong —?"

"She's got spoon medicine from Uncle Doctor. Tonic," Dabney said importantly, his voice dropping to normal.

While her father shouldered out into the wind again,

88

Tolly freshened the open fire under the kettle of water that hung there. Dabney, between renewed moans, pointed out where the medicine was kept, and she poured a spoonful of it into Aunt Emmeline's mouth. She was trying to get the strong tea down her throat by spoonfuls when a hammering on the door called her to unbar it. Dr. Lincoln and his faithful medicine bag and a great blast of wind pushed their way in together.

"Well, young lady," he scolded Aunt Emmeline, when the closed door brought a blessed hush. "What have you been up to this time? Think you're a gal-chile, running out in a wind like this?" As he scolded, his eyes were keen on her face, and his hands, long and strong like Sojer's, were gently feeling her arms, her legs, her chest. "Look like you too old and tough to break!" he growled, and Tolly gave a little sigh of relief. "Where do you hurt, Aunt Em?"

"Easier — say — where don't — I hurt," she replied with a flash of humor, though her voice was almost too faint to hear. "But that boy-chile?" Her eyes turned painfully in Dabney's direction.

"He'll live to be hanged. — Now, now, we'll tend to him in a minute. Age before beauty," the doctor muttered mechanically. "First I hurt you some more, Aunt Em —" Already he had his sterile hypodermic out, pinched up a fold of skin on her fleshless arm, and jabbed deep.

"Didn't hurt — now the boy-chile —"

"I tell you he's fine as silk." He laid down her withered

arm and patted it as he drew the sleeve over it. "I'll just give the rascal a good wash and some stinging mercurochrome —"

"How the boy-baby?" Aunt Emmeline whispered again as he worked over the child's cuts and scratches. She was barely holding open her eyes, which went shut while they looked at her.

"Out like a light," Tolly said. "Uncle Doctor, do you think — ?"

"If she was anybody but an islander," Dr. Lincoln said gravely, "I'd think a frail little piece in her middle eighties couldn't stand such a blow. Don't know what it is about us. Go on short rations too much of the time. Diet not balanced. But we've got something solid in us. Used to say that old age was the fifth greatest cause of death on St. Helena."

Tolly blew her nose hard. "Can I nurse her?"

"Sure thing, if that's what you want, Jemmeline. That is if your father says it's okay." He looked inquiringly at Mr. Tolliver, who had just entered.

"Fine, fine, daughter," he agreed, patting Dabney's round young head, all crisped over with curls. "At any rate till we can get Nurse Jenny. I'll take this boy home and inform your mother of the situation. She will know what to send you in the way of garments and toiletries."

11

ALL NIGHT the storm raged around the cabin, while Tolly gave thanks that the Penn boys had built and anchored it so stoutly. Sometimes the wind turned round and puffed malevolently down the chimney, till smoke and ashes billowed into the room and Aunt Emmeline's strings of egg shells — hung from the mantel to make the hens lay — blew straight out. If the chimney had been the older clay and stick style — Tolly shuddered at the thought.

Fighting his way back, her father brought twice as much nourishing soup as two people could use, especially when one was still under sedation. He brought bedding for a pallet on the floor, and Tolly's nightgown, robe, and slippers, as well as fresh things to put on in the morning. Ellen had sent her writing portfolio and a new paperback.

Tolly fussed to and fro, counting Aunt Emmeline's breaths and watching for any change in that claylike pallor. She was thankful when Dr. Lincoln pounded the door again, calling his name to reassure her. Again the invasion of the cabin by the wind and the returning quiet.

When he took Aunt Emmeline's pulse and laid a hand on her forehead, she roused at last, and looked at them with eyes gradually clearing.

"The boy-baby?" she asked.

"You and your boy-baby! He can be purely thankful if he never has anything worse than his scratches," the doctor said.

"Oh, Aunt Emmeline," Tolly begged, bending over her. "How do you feel?"

"Like I flying right up to the great white throne," Aunt Emmeline whispered with a little smile. "First thing I ask the good Lawd is will he please take this aching body off of me —" Her gray face twisted with pain —

"We'll not wait for the Lord," Dr. Lincoln said briskly. "We'll take the pain, not the body, though." Again he had filled the syringe and again he found a place for the needle in a fold of emaciated arm.

"Aunt Emmeline," Tolly pleaded, "don't talk about going to heaven. We can't spare you yet."

"I sho' be glad efn I can give my life fo' that little boy-chile — same as — the first teacher at Penn — give her life — for usn." Again her voice drifted off to silence.

"She could make it. Or not," Dr. Lincoln answered Tolly's wide, questioning eyes. "Anyway, she's had a good life. She's rejoiced in the beauties of the earth, she's loved and been loved, she's served, and looks homeward to a beloved Lord —"

It was still early when Tolly ate her soup and tidily

washed the few dishes. Aunt Emmeline slept, but the wind, though diminishing in fury, made a hubbub that prevented normal sleep. Tolly read awhile, stopping every few minutes to look at her patient. Then she contemplated the writing kit Ellen had sent.

Rich Corwin had brought Sojer more definitely to her mind. She had promised to write to him, even if she did not say how soon or how often. She might as well get it over with.

"Dear Sojer," she wrote, "you couldn't guess where I am tonight. At Aunt Emmeline's, over near Old Penn. It's still blowing great guns, but nothing like this morning, when the big live oak lost several of its limbs and might have caused my little brother to lose some of his, or even his life, if it hadn't been for Aunt Emmeline. She risked her own to save his. That's why I'm here, nursing her till they can get someone better. Dr. Lincoln says she has a fifty-fifty chance. I don't know but she comes right next to Papa and Mama and Ellen and Dabney, for me."

The mention of Dr. Lincoln would hurt Sojer, but didn't he deserve to be hurt?

Other sick and injured on the island needed Nurse Jenny, and Tolly stayed two more days. On the third day Aunt Emmeline was in less pain, and Dr. Lincoln reduced her sedation. She was able to talk a little to Tolly, and to Tolly's father and mother when they came with supplies and inquiries.

"We must coax her appetite," Mrs. Tolliver softly told Tolly at the door. "Dr. Lincoln says it will be a matter of getting her enough nourishment so it isn't all out-go and no in-come."

That same afternoon a different knock sounded on the blue door frame. Now that the wind was only a strong breeze, Tolly had thrown wide the doors and shutters. She went quickly to answer the rapping, and looked up into an unexpected face. Resting a hand against the frame, Rich Corwin stood smiling down at her.

"Why, good afternoon," she stammered. "Why — how did you know I was here?"

"Oh, I just came calling on the lady of the house," he said solemnly. "Always did fancy Aunt Emmeline. Seriously — you asked me to phone before I came, but the phones on the islands are mostly down, so I came over to your-own house, and they told me where I'd find you. I hope I don't intrude."

Hastily Tolly stood aside, realizing that she had not even asked him in. "Excuse me," she said, laughing. "These last few days — well, Aunt Emmeline would say I was an 'unmannersable somebody,' for true."

Aunt Emmeline's thin, husky voice saved her further excuses, but did not save her embarrassment.

"Sojer!" she cried, with a gladness of welcome that sent the hot blood surging into Tolly's face. "Sojer, I too glad."

With a quirk of lips and a lift of brows for Tolly,

Rich strode over to the old woman's bed. "Must I say I'm sorry I'm not Sojer, Aunt Emmeline? I'm Rich Corwin from over at Lady's Island. I knew you when I was only so high."

Tolly noticed, even in her confusion, that Rich made his manners for the island woman like a true island boy, bowing politely at her bedside.

"Rich Corwin," Aunt Emmeline said slowly. "You favor yo' pa and yo' ma, both two. It's a long time since I see you, but I know you and yo' granny and yo' great-granny befo' you." She stopped for want of breath, her eyes still searching Rich's fine face.

After he had talked with her a little, she closed her eyes. "Scuse me efn I rest awhile," she said, with delicate courtesy leaving the young people free to talk to each other.

"Will it be all right if we sit on the porch, Aunt Emmeline? Not to disturb you with our chatter? Isn't there something I can get you first?"

"Nothing, I thank you. Just a little small nap," Aunt Emmeline murmured.

Tolly began an uncomfortable explanation. "Sojer — was a friend at Fisk. A premed. Aunt Emmeline liked the idea of him. Mostly because he wanted to practice on the islands."

"I know." Rich sighed. "Your little sis filled me in on Sojer. Showed me the yearbook — all those pictures. Especially that one, 'Couple most likely to succeed.'

Well, I would have thought they were a lot of blind men there at Fisk if they had let a girl like you go clean through without being anyway pinned. And this Sojer's a good-looking guy. Looks good, too."

"But he isn't so good," Tolly found herself saying in an almost inaudible rush of words. "I thought he was, but he isn't. So it's all over. — Oh, I'm not crying about him. I am not." Indignantly she dashed away the tears. "I'm just so worried about Aunt Em I can cry about nothing."

"Suppose it wouldn't help any to tell me about it?" Rich asked gently. "About this Sojer?"

Though Tolly would have said it was the last thing that would help, she found herself pouring out the whole story. "I just couldn't ever trust him again," she finished. "And him with a real gift of healing —"

"Poor Sojer. Loses his dreams of a profession and a way of life. Loses a girl like you. Now what will he do about picking up the pieces?"

"That's not up to me," Tolly said, a hardness creeping into her voice. "I did my best to help him, and what did it get me? Nothing but disappointment. Oh, I'll go on and do all I can for my people. But I dare anyone to try to get close to me again. Some people can stand it, but it tears me to pieces." She blinked back a new flood of tears. "After this I'll work with my head and not so much with my heart. Maybe that's what is best for our people anyway."

Rich was looking at her with eyes as steady as Sojer's used to be. "Seems like work is kind of dead without plenty of heart in it."

Again they were interrupted, this time by a cough from within the cabin. Tolly answered its summons, and in a moment came to the door. "She would like to see you again," she said.

Rich stood at the bedside, smiling down at the old woman.

"You — you got yo' deeploma and all?" she asked. When he nodded, she said, "Reckon you gwine off the islands, then, like mostly all our chillen."

"No, Aunt Emmeline. Soon as I pass the examination I mean to settle down on Lady's. I aim to be the best lawyer in these parts. Like enough I'll starve, but I'll starve trying."

"One thing fo' true — you don't got to starve on these islands. Plenty s'rimps and oysters and crabs and —" Her voice trailed away.

"Rabbits, squirrels, coons —" Tolly continued the list.

"I too glad you stay on the islands," Aunt Emmeline repeated. "Maybe you law for Mather when they need it."

"Aunt Em loves Mather right next to Old Penn," Tolly said.

"My mother likewise," Rich said. "She teaches over there whenever they need her."

"Sho' wish this honey chile teach there," Aunt Emmeline said wistfully. Her eyes were so misty with longing that Tolly would have said almost anything to lighten them.

"Oh, Aunt Em, if they ask me, I will. If they ask me," she repeated. She did not think it necessary to say, "If they ask me again."

12

AFTERWARD Tolly wondered whether the island grape-vine, which seemed to carry news uncannily, had taken those words of hers to Mather.

At the end of the week, Dr. Lincoln thought Aunt Emmeline well enough to be left alone, since the Tollivers would visit her every day and he would pay her an occasional call.

Tolly had hardly settled into her own home again when a letter came from the president of Mather. Their English teacher must be given leave of absence because of illness in her family. Would Tolly be able to modify her previous refusal and act as substitute?

"Oh, heavens!" Tolly moaned. "Now I've got to spend a semester, probably, at Mather!"

"You've got to? Why?" her mother inquired. "I thought you meant to apply at St. Helena. And it's time you did, even with the teacher shortage."

"I passed my word to Aunt Emmeline," Tolly admitted. "I never thought they'd ask me again. But I passed my word."

In that same stack of mail she had looked for another letter, one she had expected would fly back to her as soon as hers had reached its goal. Instead, there was one from Langston.

"Well, thank goodness there is nothing from Sojer," she declared loudly to Ellen, who was dimpling over a letter from Orbert, and caressing her blue-black hair in a way that seemed to indicate what she was reading.

"You're thankful not to hear from Sojer? That poor boy. Why don't you write to him again? Just to show him you don't hate him."

"I've done what I promised. I don't see a speck of use knocking myself out to think of things to say, things that are true and yet not hard on him."

"I suppose you'll write to Langston, though."

"It's easy to write to Langston."

"And easy to date that Rich Corwin, I suppose." Ellen's tone was a mixture of deprecation and envy. "Well, anyway, it gives me a chance at a little fun. Now let me read my letter."

Tolly did write an acceptance to Mather, and she did answer Langston, making a conscious effort to be sophisticated. To Sojer she did not write; neither did she hear from him. July passed, and August, and still no letter.

"It's beyond me," Ellen fumed, "how you can just keep still, not knowing whether he's dead or alive. If I'd dated anyone as much as you dated Sojer, and if he worshiped the ground I walked on — well, I can't see myself dropping him like a hot potato, just because he made one mistake. As we were saying before, the Bible says, 'Let him that is without sin cast the first stone!'"

It was so funny to hear little fly-up-the-creek Ellen quoting Scripture at her, Tolly, that she giggled in spite of the dreariness of the subject. Ellen glared.

"Well, if it will make you feel any better," Tolly promised, "I will stretch a point and write to Sojer again. Oh, why couldn't he have been as straight and decent as Rich?"

But she was thinking that every time Rich seemed to her especially fine, Sojer seemed even finer. Maybe it was just because their four years of close companionship had made him a part of her life — a part that had been wrenched out of it with such sudden violence that the wound was slow to heal.

"Oh, I know there's nothing against Rich," Ellen went on fussing. "But how can you condemn a person for just one slip? Besides, you have to compare Sojer's raising with Rich's."

Tolly sighed. "Yes, it was what went before that made the trouble for Sojer — that kept him from succeeding at Fisk. It was the ghastly poor education he'd had in elementary and high. That's what makes me furious with the white people," she cried. It was the point she returned to, over and over again.

Their father had been apparently buried in a book, there on the veranda, where they had all sought any stirring of breeze in the moist August heat that lay upon them like a wet blanket. Subconsciously Tolly had noted that his pages had ceased turning.

Now he cleared his throat and spoke slowly. "As we

have quoted before, daughter, 'It is better to light one candle than to curse the darkness.' You need to remember, also, that many white people have been lighting candles for us, some of them for a good long spell. Look at Old Penn. Look at Mather. I don't know but it's past time we took more responsibility for lighting our own candles. This is our country. We've got to give to it as well as take from it. Light a candle. Light a thousand candles."

"What would you call the sit-ins and other nonviolent protests?" Tolly asked him.

"I don't quite know. First I thought that since things were moving, we'd better not interfere. But it takes a long time. Look when it was that the Supreme Court ruled for integration — eight years ago, wasn't it? And in the seventeen segregated states and the District of Columbia, 92.4 per cent are still segregated. 100 per cent segregated in our own state. So maybe we should do a little gentle pushing, ourselves."

Tolly nodded rather absently, for she had been thinking what she would write to Sojer this time. When she settled down to the task, she made the letter somewhat easier and less critical. She certainly didn't want to be the holier-than-thou type that Ellen had suggested. But she was careful not to imply any possibility of a return to their old friendship. And she did tell him about Rich Corwin. She worked so hard on the writing that her face and neck were wet and her dress stuck to the back of her chair when she sat back to read her own words over.

Sojer would not have been alarmed about Rich, Tolly thought as she sealed and stamped the letter, if he could have known how slowly Rich moved in matters romantic. Though she was only nineteen, Tolly had seen several boys make greater strides in a week than Rich in a summer. It was just as well, until she could get Sojer completely out of her mind. Yet she hoped Rich would say something a degree or two warmer before he bade her good-by.

The time for farewell came fast, for Mather opened early, and Tolly had her clothes to get ready, courses of study Dr. Andrews had sent her to review, daily visits to Aunt Emmeline, and a few hours weekly at the Community Center, all in the heavy August heat.

Rich had asked if he might come over on her last night at home. He too would be going away, to law school and a job.

The early September evening was dreamily lovely, rich with flower fragrances. Swing, rockers, porch railing were all occupied when Rich arrived. Mr. and Mrs. Tolliver talked with him longer than Tolly thought necessary. Perhaps reading her silence, they finally remembered urgent tasks. Papa had promised to go to a praise house that night, and suggested that Ellen and Dabney might like to go along. When Dabney politely declined, Papa grasped his collar with deceptive playfulness and steered him out to the car, yipping protests. Mama had light-bread ready to bake, arranging so as not to keep the oven going during the hot day.

The porch fell very silent, except for the creak-cree-eak of the gently swaying swing and the rhythmic rise and fall of the cicada song.

"I always loved cicadas," Tolly said, rather desperately. "And fireflies. Don't you?"

"Hm, yes," Rich agreed. "Tolly—"

Tolly tingled Whatever was coming, she was not ready. "Did you use to catch the poor things and keep them in bottles?" she asked hurriedly.

"Bottles? What bottles?" Rich lapsed into a dense silence without listening for a reply.

Again the heavy hush.

"Tolly —" Again she held her breath — "Tolly, how did you find Aunt Emmeline today?"

Tolly let out her breath in a sigh that held something like exasperation. "Aunt Emmeline is doing as well as could possibly be expected. If only she had someone of her own —"

"You treat her as if you were her own," Rich mused. "Funny you aren't afraid of involving yourself with her."

"Why, that's different. We've always had Aunt Emmeline. And she's such a lamb. And we can't expect to have her forever. And then, as Papa says, the last bit of old St. Helena will be gone."

"But you're not letting yourself in for a lifetime of commitment. Not for anyone," Rich said, in a funny, uneven voice.

"Why — what a horrid thing to say!"

"I'm sorry. It wasn't nice. I'm sort of upset tonight, leaving — everybody."

"But I suppose you're going back to somebody," Tolly said, against her own firm resolve. "Of course there's a girl in Illinois."

Rich managed a laugh. "Lots of girls in Illinois. As for a special one, well, might be and might not."

So that explained his caution!

"Maybe I'm too much like that old song," he said: " 'I want a girl / Just like the girl / Who married dear old Dad.' Well, I don't exactly. Yet it was sort of startling to meet you, Tolly, because you're Mother's type, tall and slim and with those wide-set eyes. But I'll settle for someone warm and outgoing like Mother. Any old time I will."

"She must be a very superior person," Tolly said stiffly.

"Yes, she is, and that's another thing in which you're like her."

Again Tolly held her breath, not knowing whether she wanted him to go on or not. He didn't. He said, had she read *To Kill a Mockingbird?* And what did she think of it?

And without returning to the really interesting topic again, they talked on and on, about books, and Freedom Rides, and sit-ins, and Martin Luther King, and Gandhi.

Father's car came chugging back, and Dabney evaded him and perched on the railing, and Mama brought out frosty lemonade and sticky buns for them all.

A half-hour later, Tolly walked down to the gate with Rich. He pulled from his pocket a flat box that was evidently chocolates and handed it to her, looking at her for a long, still moment in the light that streamed palely from the open door.

"Well, good-by," he said huskily, "for now." He went quickly through the gate and jumped into his car.

"Did he propose? Did you accept?" Ellen asked excitedly, when Tolly returned to the porch.

"My goodness, no, he didn't come within a mile of it," Tolly answered with a fairly successful laugh. "I thought he'd never go. No terminal facilities. And I have to get up at the crack of dawn."

Of course she was glad he hadn't proposed. She was by no means free of Sojer.

Yet it gave her a forlorn feeling, that he, whom she came near liking so much, had evidently made up his mind not to like her.

13

SEVERAL years had passed since Tolly had seen much of Mather. In her junior year in the high school her work had been so good that she was invited to enter Fisk in the fall as an Early Entrant. Her parents were reluctant, wanting her to stay as long as possible in Mather, but Tolly's eagerness to shorten her undergraduate years had persuaded them to consent.

Everything had changed in the four years, even Beaufort, which had so long stood firm as a little "unreconstructed" Southern city. Of course there were still old buildings: one like a Greek temple, put up before the War Between the States, and now used by the University of South Carolina at Beaufort; and St. Helena Episcopal Church, dating back to before the Revolution; and numberless fine old ante-bellum houses. Behind some of these stood houses which had been their kitchens and their slave quarters.

As they drove over the mile or so of blacktop leading to Mather, the changes were apparent. Little of the old stretch of deep woods along the bay was left unbroken. It was being divided for building lots and soon other comfortable houses would join the many new ones that sat back among their tremendous trees as if they had always been there. There were a few apartment houses, too, strangely modern amid the old.

And the campus was as much changed. The gate, with its white iron trellis and its letters MATHER SCHOOL across the top, still arched over the walk leading from the buildings on one side of the highway to those on the other. That gate had become through long years a sort of symbol of the old school.

The greenery and the flowers were much the same as always: those live oaks, each a world in itself, and the magnolias and pecans. Though each year's storms and the hurricanes which so often struck the sea islands took their toll of the beloved trees, their number hardly seemed less. The campus had always been a place of enchantment, with glimpses of the bay seen through filmy curtains of gray moss.

But the buildings! Only two of the ancient structures remained, built in the 1860's, from the lumber of the Union Army's barracks, floated down the waterway for the use of the brand-new school. The immediately preceding years had brought an anonymous money gift that had allowed the erection of three adequate modern buildings, brick like all the rest of those that had replaced the antiquated clapboard structures.

And more boys were to be seen on the campus. Even in Tolly's years there the junior college had been added, open to boys as well as girls. Junior college had grown, and the number of boys in the high school had increased.

It was more fun than with girls only, Tolly frankly admitted to herself. And though scholastically she would be much further advanced than any of the students, she was no older than many of them. She supposed a teacher would not be expected to date students; but there were the night classes, and the same restrictions might not apply to them.

Leaving her father in the car, Tolly ran up the steps of the hall that housed the administrative offices, and stood before the little swinging gate that closed the president's doorway. In a moment the president looked up from her desk and then sat back to smile at her new substitute.

Dr. Eloise was a small woman with silvery hair and smiling blue eyes. Tolly thought those eyes and the upcurving mouth often had a private joke with each other, a joke that was oftenest about the president herself. It was a reassuring expression, especially since the eyes could look into and through a culprit with such cool clarity, and the smiling mouth could be so decisively unsmiling.

The treasurer and registrar across the hall had been one of the several who knew Tolly as a student, and she joined her welcome to Dr. Eloise's. It would be a strange experience to be here as the colleague of these women and some of her former teachers.

There was no room left in the dormitories, Dr. Eloise told her, the enrollment being so much greater than before. Tolly was to have one of the two rooms upstairs in

109

Mather Cottage. Another teacher was using the smaller of the rooms, so Tolly might take the larger one, usually a guest room. The cottage was one of the two earliest buildings, home of the founder of the school in the hard, impoverished days immediately after the war, almost a hundred years ago. On the ground floor both Dr. Eloise and Miss Long, the registrar, had their suites of rooms.

Tolly dashed out to her father's car, suddenly pleased and excited. "I'll like being in Mather Cottage," she exulted, as he drove on and parked behind the rambling structure.

Her father was not so sure. Carrying her suitcases through the inviting screened porch and up the steep stairs, he studied the place thoughtfully. "Hate to see a conflagration start here," he said, shaking his head.

"Fire extinguishers handy on the wall. And look, these rooms are even quainter than ours at home. The little one has kept even the heavy plank doors. Maybe that's why Miss Long chose it. Dr. Eloise invited you to stay to luncheon," she remembered, as he set down her luggage and went to a window.

"I'll stop and express my appreciation." He was resting his hands on a weathered sill and looking down at the porch roof below it, as if estimating the drop to the ground. "But I must be hastening on my way, for I have an appointment in Beaufort before I return home."

"What business in Beaufort?" Tolly inquired.

He waved his hat in a dismissing gesture. "Need to see a member of the interracial committee. About voting registration." His tone was somber, as if he did not relish his task. "Outside Beaufort mostly, Beaufort always having been pretty reasonable about letting the Negro vote. I don't know but getting us to use our franchise is important right now, more than sit-ins and such."

Tolly walked with him to the office and then to his car, standing beside his window when he had got in. He patted her hand, resting on the door. "I commend you, daughter," he said. "I believe this is a superior opportunity as regards the good you may accomplish. As you have so often remarked, the gap between the early education of the Negro in the Deep South and the requirements in white graduate schools — and even white undergraduate schools — is one of the most stubborn obstacles to school integration. Mather, with its well-prepared faculty, gives solid preparation — helps bridge the abyss. Working here, you are in truth lighting those candles."

"But in my heart I'm still cursing the darkness," Tolly breathed in a stubborn undertone. "No, I won't let on, Papa. I can hide it for a semester."

She somehow dreaded to see him go, and watched his car as long as it was in sight. She could always identify it, for it had started out a beautiful deep maroon, but now its rear end and doors had faded to a sickly plum color. In all the recent accession of cars to St. Helena Island, Papa's was one of the shabbiest, except for the hot rods and jalopies of some of the kids. The great number of glossy cars in all the pastel colors was one of the most apparent signs of the change in the islands. Papa, with the small salary from his church, even with Mama's teacher's salary added, had had to figure and skimp to keep two daughters in college at the same time.

When the plum color was lost to her eyes, she hurried back into the office, and to Miss Long's swinging gate. She had slowed her step as she came in the door, and she made her expression nonchalant, her tone laughingly apologetic.

"I suppose the mail comes in about the same time it used to, Miss Long?" she asked, when the treasurer looked up inquiringly. "I thought probably. I wouldn't be likely to have anything yet, but I'll just locate myself. Would I have a pigeonhole in the boxes down the hall here?"

"Right, Tolly," assented Miss Long as she went back to her work. "It's going to be hard to remember about calling you Miss Tolliver," she said, lifting her eyes again. "I'll try when the girls are around — and the boys."

Tolly laughed politely and swung her long stride down the hall and around the corner to the small bank of boxes. T — would be near the lower right-hand end. Yes, her name had already been thumbtacked there, but the pigeonhole was empty.

She went out soberly and started toward Mather Cottage. She was silly to be disappointed, but she had mentioned to both Langston and Sojer, as well as to other correspondents, that she would be getting her mail at Mather for a while. Likely enough Langston had someone else on his mind by this time. And maybe what she had written about Rich had made Sojer feel that there was no more hope at all. Yet she had really expected her last letter to draw an immediate reply. Of course she was glad to have Sojer withdrawing, since their friendship could have no future. If she were fickle, she wouldn't have this ache in her heart, this pressure, as of tears waiting to spring out of her eyes.

No, and she wouldn't have this silly shortness of breath whenever she caught sight of someone tall and broad-shouldered and young. — As now, when a loose-jointed figure swung out from the side of Moor Hall ahead of her.

The figure had not the least real resemblance to Sojer's. It hadn't the powerful column of throat nor the splendid carriage. And the long arms swung only slightly, without Sojer's telltale manner. And when he turned and started back, cracking his knuckles as if he had forgotten something, she saw that his face was as unlike Sojer's as it was possible for a face to be. It was too large at the brows and too small at the chin, though engagingly piquant.

Perhaps because of the intentness of her gaze, he smiled, tugging at his curly hair as at a cap. "You a stranger, too, miss?" he asked hopefully. "You know where at we supposed to go?"

"To register? High school registration is tomorrow, and junior college next week. But back yonder's the office. They'll answer your questions better than I can. I just came."

"High school?" he asked, still hopeful.

Tolly hesitated, laughing. She foresaw many such occasions. "Well, no, I'm on the staff this semester. Just substituting for an English teacher on leave," she added, to make it less formidable.

"Nobody ever believe you old enough," the boy said solemnly. "Scuse it if it sound bold, but it sure a treat to mind a teacher like you. High school?" The hope persisted.

"Both," Tolly admitted. "English."

"And of the two subjects this child needs the mostest, that there English is the both of them," he said fervently.

"Well, if you're likely to be my pupil, we may as well introduce ourselves. I'm Jane Emmeline Tolliver, from St. Helena. I suppose, being a teacher, I'll have to be Miss Tolliver."

"Yes, ma'am. Sho' right please to meet you, miss. Me, I'm Gabriel Vesey, from Virginia. And it's plain Gabe, since I'm a scholar, and a dumb one."

"Gabriel Vesey," Tolly considered, as he fell into step with her. "It's a grand name. Sounds familiar, somehow."

He laughed, a surprisingly high-pitched peal, yet pleasant. "I knowed you'd recognize it. I'm his great-great-great-grand."

Light dawned in Tolly's memory. "The one who led the big slave insurrection," she said, as if she had known it all along. She studied his face thoughtfully. This tall gangling boy with the oddly elfish face could hardly have looked less like that fiery, invincible leader of bygone days.

"Yes, ma'am, he sho' was my great-granddaddy," he said, as if perhaps he read doubt in her eyes.

They had reached Mather Cottage, and Tolly halted, smiling at him. "This is where I'm living right now."

Gabe's curiously light brown eyes seemed to be taking in the deep shady porch with its look of comfort. "Sho' nice," he said. "Good day to you, miss."

Next day Tolly helped with registration, and found herself watching for Gabe. "Are you getting boy-crazy, like your little sis?" she scolded herself. "No, it's that something about Gabe that reminds me of Sojer. And he needs coaching as badly as Sojer did."

His handwriting strengthened this belief, and some spelling as amazing as Sojer's used to be. He seemed aware of his shortcomings. "Miss," he asked, after waiting around till she got up to join the other teachers at lunch, "Miss, do you reckon I can do the work?"

Those light brown eyes glowed with painful intensity, and the forehead had lines deeper than his age.

"You'll have to work pretty hard, Gabe. But I'm sure some of your teachers will want to give you extra help."

"Miss, would you — ?"

Here she was, in danger of fresh involvement. "I'm only here as a substitute," she warned. "Of course I shan't mind giving you a lift now and then —"

"Miss — I knowed it when first I seen you. You just too good."

"That," Tolly said decisively, "is what I'm not — at least in the future. Excuse me, Gabe. I want to see if I got any mail."

She hadn't.

After luncheon classes assembled, and Gabe was in her first English class, face puckered but eyes shining. He lingered when the session was over. She could feel his presence near her desk, and for a moment busied herself with the roll. But she couldn't continue to ignore him. "Something, Gabe?" she inquired crisply.

"Yes'm. Is they some book will help me learn proper talk quicker?"

His was such an old child's face, perched high on the tall body. It gazed at her with such an intense anxiety, brightened by the hope that seemed built into him. She would have to do something.

"Gabe, I'll study over it. I'll try to find something—"

Thanking her repeatedly, he shambled out as her high school senior class began to assemble. First to enter was a girl of medium height and build, almost as pretty as Ellen, but more briskly competent.

She gave her name. "I'm Rosabelle Gibbs, Miss Tolliver." She eyed the young teacher appreciatively. "Miss, it looks like you'd have your hands full with the one that just went out."

"Rosabelle, my job load is going to be heavy enough without that. Maybe you could lend a hand yourself."

"He's sort of cute, isn't he?" Rosabelle said thoughtfully. "Even if he is straight from the sticks."

14

THE DAY passed, and the week, and registration for junior college. Some of the college freshmen had finished high school at Mather, and some were from other schools, far and wide. One boy came from New York City and one girl from Africa. Twin boys were from Haiti. Unlike Tolly's earliest memories of Mather, its student body dressed in a way not noticeably different from students anywhere. Few looked frightened, as if they had entered a world too strange for them. None spoke with the broad Gullah dialect of the region, formerly so common. Yet Tolly had picked out a half-dozen who would need intensive coaching if they were to have any hope of further education.

"That little Flora in my junior class in high," Tolly said to the president as they sat down to the table in the dining hall one evening, "why, the girl can't read! It's no wonder she has trouble getting her lessons. I should say she read at about third-grade level."

"She's the girl over at the third table, with her feet wound round her chair legs, isn't she?" Dr. Eloise sighed. "She is one of a family of twelve, and a neighbor felt that Mather was her only chance for development. This neighbor says she's naturally neat and capable around sick people. But in the school where she's had to go she's just been passed from one grade to another, whether she had learned anything or not. I'll see if I can squeeze in a half-hour a day and teach her to read."

She did not look at Tolly, and it was Tolly's turn to sigh. "Your light is always on when I turn mine out, Dr. Eloise. I'll see what I can do with Flora. But where do I start? Dr. Eloise, I asked her to read that household favorite from Longfellow. I have known it all my life like a next-door neighbor: you know, the one about the murmuring pines and the hemlocks standing like druids of old, with beards that descend and all that. Well, Flora not only couldn't begin to pronounce 'hemlocks' and 'druids' and 'descend' — she didn't have the faintest notion what they meant. But I'll try my hand at it."

"Now if it were only her table manners," the president murmured, "they seem to get those by osmosis, the bright ones."

"It didn't take her long to catch on to making a bed in the infirmary," Mrs. Saunders, the nurse, chimed in.

"But words and abstract ideas — they just don't absorb them in a month. Or a year. But there's an example of growth for you."

A bell had tapped, and a tall girl stood to make an announcement. Her small head was confidently high and she spoke clearly and with assurance. "The junior college sophs are sponsoring an oyster roast Saturday night.

All the oysters you can eat, fifty cents. Or hot dogs, if anyone is so queer as to prefer them. Crackers and cocoa, too. Please make your reservation by Thursday, with Miss Long or me. And go to the gymnasium-auditorium to pay your fifty cents and get your ticket pinned on. Let's make it a great big success." With a bright, quick smile she added, "We juniors mean to make a class gift that will put all other class gifts in the shade. The uncle of one of our number is getting us the oysters free. Please do help make it a success."

"You could hardly believe the kind of house this Belle came from," Dr. Eloise said with a commendatory smile at Belle, as the girl sat down. "She even had to be taught about regular baths and clean clothes. It makes you wonder at the glory of the human soul. Now she can fit into a Northern college with little trouble. And her grades are so good that she has already been promised a scholarship in one."

Tolly looked from Belle, sitting erect but not too erect at the table, to Flora, shoveling food into a low-hung face. "Miracles do happen here. But — a high school girl who can't read Longfellow —"

"She's never been exposed to it — or to much of anything else."

"But she's not stupid. The way she catches on to making beds —" Mrs. Saunders repeated.

The day of the oyster roast came, warm enough, Tolly commented to one of her classes, to make an ice cream social more inviting. But evening brought a tinge of autumn coolness, and Tolly ran back to her room for a sweater. Gabe stood behind the cottage, hands in pockets, facing the bay at the east edge of the campus. He turned as Tolly came out, and waved an awkward hand toward the afterglow that painted sky and water.

"An hour ago," he said, "you should seen it, Miss Tolly. When it look thataway, I calls it the Power and the Glory."

"The Power and the Glory. I like that, Gabe." Tolly studied the strange, wistful face. You never could tell.

Dark thickened fast, while the prospective oyster eaters gathered at the gymnasium-auditorium, which still filled Tolly with admiration. It was so right and adequate, after the years of Mather's making-do. At a summons by a messenger, they all trooped out to the big barbecue fireplace, with its dim figures hovering around, feeding the flames.

It was a magic sort of scene that Tolly stood watching, with Miss Long, and one of the tall young physical ed teachers, who was not many years older than Tolly.

Broad sheets of iron had been laid across the fireplace, and panfuls of oysters dumped on the iron, in horny gray masses. As soon as the shells opened, they were brushed off into a basket and passed to the eaters.

"Teacher, if you set down I fetch yo' oysters," said Gabe, who was hovering near.

"Thank you, Gabe. —Doesn't it make you feel a generation older?" she asked the physical ed teacher, as they sat down at one of the picnic tables, with Mrs. Saunders, the nurse, and Miss Long.

As the darkness deepened, those at the tables fumbled in the black shadows for the hot sauces and the crackers that had been set out, and burned their fingers on the heavy shells and their mouths on the oysters which they pried loose and dropped on their tongues. They were so sweet-flavored and delicate that Tolly ate on and on, before she finally wriggled out between table and bench and retreated, with the coach and the nurse, to keep a watchful eye on the students.

"They think we are regular hawks, the way we chaperon them." Mrs. Saunders spoke with an amused crispness.

Again Tolly wished that her camera could catch more than was possible for it, or that she could paint a picture that would capture the charm of the scene. Smoke streamed up from the chimney, streaked with flames and interspersed with showers of sparks. It made a tunnel of red light that reached up into the dense blackness of the great trees, and silvered the pennants of Spanish moss as it danced fantastically up and down.

"It sho' pretty," Gabe said at her side. "Miss, you meet up with Melom yet?" Near him stood a strong, short figure, whose lustrous eyes seemed to catch the firelight.

"Melom? Oh, yes. He is in one of my classes."

"He don't need no help with his English, like I do,"

Gabe said admiringly. "He talk like a book."

"More correctly than most of us," Tolly agreed.

"In that mission school in my country," explained Melom, "we have teachers from England. They wish that we speak like them."

His clipped British accent accorded with the glossy darkness of his face, its smoothness broken only by deep scars on each cheek, evidently cut in a design that had meaning.

"You have stopped wearing those white silk robes, Melom," Tolly said rather regretfully. "They were handsome."

"An African I met when I reached America gave them to me," he said soberly. "He told me that in your country they would cause me to be politely treated, while in plain clothes I should be scorned as a servant. Here at the school I find it not so."

"Tell me about your coming here," Tolly coaxed.

Gabe and another student pulled up a bench, and Tolly and her fellow staff members sat down while a group of students gathered round them. After a momentary hesitation, Melom told.

He had lived twelve miles from the English mission school and had walked the distance twice a day. One American teacher had been especially interested in him, and told him that if he were in America he could go to college. So Melom said, "I will go to America." — Just like that, Tolly thought. — One day he started to walk to America, barefoot and wearing his school shirt and shorts. He carried meal enough to last a week, and thought that would be long enough.

He walked two thousand miles. Through hostile country he walked all night and hid during the day, though in the darkness it was harder to avoid dangerous snakes.

On and on, with the coast seeming to recede before him, he tramped for more than a year, stopping only long enough to work for some food after the week's supply was gone. When he reached a seaport he found a new difficulty, the problem of getting a visa. But a local missionary telegraphed to a small mission school in America, and the reply was almost immediate: Mather would accept Melom as a student, and give him a working scholarship.

That answer took care of his visa, and Melom signed on a ship headed for America and worked his passage to the United States. From that point, he said, it was easy: he had only to hitch-hike to South Carolina.

Gabe had stirred restlessly in the darkness and he burst out when Melom paused. "I think I got it plenty hard. Sho' look easy, alongside this fellow."

"I had a college classmate," Tolly said as if her thoughts had crept into speech without her planning it. "He'd had to work his way, digging ditches, doing most anything. His early schooling had been practically worthless, his father wouldn't help him, and all his mother could do was wash clothes and pick cotton, so Sojer could save his earnings for college. But he couldn't make the grade."

"His mother helped him," Melom said soberly. "Mine had too many children to feed, so she threw me away. In the river. But that was okay, because an old man pulled me out before I could die."

In spite of the stark tragedy between the lines, Tolly laughed with Melom and the other listeners, marveling at the boy's strength, courage, humor.

But she thought impatiently that it took next to nothing to turn her mind back to Sojer. Now again she was tormented with wondering where he was, what he was doing, why he had not answered her letters, whether it was because he had entirely given up hope.

"You go far away in your mind," Gabe complained. "Twice I ask you would you by this time like a few more oysters?"

Laughing, she asked his pardon and, calling to Rosa-belle and Flora to join them, entered into the fun again. Eagerly Gabe ran and brought great clusters of the horny gray shells, little colonies lifted from the floor of the bay. Again Tolly burned her tongue on the flavorsome morsels, and burned it even more by too hasty a sipping of hot cocoa.

She could hardly wait to get back to Mather Cottage and write to Sojer. It would empty her mind of that problem.

Three times she wrote the letter. She imagined Sojer

had found new friends, she said, as she had done. That was right. But she wished he would write just once more, and tell her how he was and what he was doing. For she would always feel like a sister to him, and would never be quite happy unless she knew he was all right.

When she had put an air mail stamp on the letter and posted it in the box inside the door of Moor Hall, she steadied herself to await the answer.

The mail would be taken to Beaufort next morning, and her letter should reach Sojer in two days. And Sojer was too "mannersable" to delay his reply when she asked it so especially. This was Saturday.

On Monday afternoon, during her English class, Tolly pictured Sojer ambling into the village post office and standing before the mail window, his head bent to look in hopefully at the postmistress. Tolly could see his face change as he took her letter. Maybe he would back off into a quiet corner before opening it. Or, just possibly, there would be a girl with him, and he would thrust it hastily into his pocket. More likely he would be alone, and would stride the miles home before reading it — stride with arm swinging.

At that point in Tolly's thought she became aware of a silence in the class, and the standing figure of Melom, with a book open in his hand and his eyes questioning her.

"Will you read the letter again, please," she said with businesslike crispness.

"The — letter, miss?"

Tolly flushed hotly. "The stanza, Melom — the stanza."

Even then her thoughts refused to march to order. Sojer would not answer the same day, she decided. He would need time to mull it over —

She dreamed of him that night, dreamed that he was trudging through snake-infested forests, her letter over his heart.

She rose, heavy-eyed, and reminded herself that he, too, would have slept poorly. He would have had to rise earlier than this — the sun was just coming up from the waters of the bay; Tolly could see its cherry red now — wherever his job might be. So he could hardly write before evening.

That would be Tuesday evening, and he could not mail the letter till Wednesday. So, if he sent it air mail, it should reach her Thursday — no, Friday.

15

THE WEEK dragged along, an unreal week, like an under-exposed movie strip. Melom and Gabe, Rosabelle and Flora, were dim figures rising, reciting — or not reciting — sitting, walking.

Thursday came. The only letter was from Ellen, who was back at Fisk, telling what fun she was having, and how Orbert was really a doll. Friday passed, with nothing better than a letter from Langston.

But Monday there was in Tolly's slender sheaf of mail one piece that made her brows knit with puzzlement. The style of stationery was her own — she prided herself on her distinctive stationery — and the address — surely it was in her vigorous slanted handwriting. Looking closer, she read through blurred eyes, "Mr. S. J. Pratt."

Staring down at it, she hurried out for the long hundred-foot walk to Mather Cottage. One of her colleagues called that she was driving to town when school was out, if Tolly wanted a ride. Rosabelle was waiting to say that if she'd like a haircut, Rosabelle would have time that evening. Gabe was lounging expectantly near the cottage, but he clapped shut his mouth when she looked unseeingly through him.

But at last she plunged out of the bright sunshine into the cool quiet of the porch, pounded up the stairs to her own room, closed the door, dropped into a chair. There she sat, her heart shaking her, as she stared stupidly at the opposite wall. What would the return of a letter mean?

It was some time before she picked it up from her lap and scrutinized the smudged blue rubber-stamp explanation for nondelivery. The line which said DECEASED was checked, but before it had been penned the words, "Believed to be."

"No," Tolly said numbly. "No, Sojer couldn't possibly be dead. Somehow I should know it, if he was not in this world any more. You don't care about a person as long as I cared about him and not know, somehow —"

She would write to his family. If his parents could not write a legible reply, surely one of his brothers or sisters could. Someone was tapping at her door; had been tapping for some time, she realized. She went and opened it. It was Miss Long from the next room, and her face twisted with concern at sight of Tolly.

"Tolly, you're sick! Come down to the nurse."

"No, I'm not — sick. I just had bad news."

"Your family?"

"No. Only someone I — used to know."

Miss Long made soft sounds of sympathy. "A good

hot supper might help. I stopped by to tell you the bell had rung."

"I — don't feel much like eating," Tolly said. "Funny, because this person didn't mean a thing to me any more. Will you give my excuses, please?"

She wanted nothing but to write that letter. She would enclose a stamped, self-addressed envelope —

"Dear Mr. and Mrs. Pratt," she wrote. "My recent letter to your son Sojourner was returned by the post office. If it is true that he —" How should she say it? Maybe the plain old way was best — "that he has died." No, she couldn't write the words. She would say, "Surely there has been a mistake. Would you please let me know? We were friends so long."

Again she had to wait, doing her tasks like a girl walking in her sleep. She kept up her work with painful care, feeling like a robot with rusty joints, and carefully outlining for herself what she must do each hour.

The reply came sooner than she expected. A penciled message, imperfectly erased here and there, it said, "Deer frend, Yrs recd. We dont know nothing sure. Sojer disappere. Boddy wash up 1 mont after. Police say it Sojer. His ma very poly. Yrs. respeck., Orlando Pratt."

Before she read this letter, Tolly had locked her door. After she read it she kept very silent, so that no one should come and knock. She was too numb, anyway, to cry out. It was as if a blow had paralyzed thought and feeling.

She sat with the letter on her lap and rocked slowly, without knowing it. "That was — not Sojer," she whispered. "No. But if he disappeared — on purpose —"

A burst of laughter from the campus told her that dinner was over. Half blindly she fumbled to unlock her door and, flashlight in hand, dash up the narrow flight of attic stairs. She pushed open the six-foot-long trap door, hooking it to a rafter till she could scramble out and let it down again.

It was dark up there. Pointing her flashlight cautiously downward, near the rough planks of the floor, she crept over to one of the deep dormer windows. There she sat cross-legged, and stared out, seeing nothing, thinking nothing, feeling nothing but a dull allover ache. But it was better to be hidden here, where they would not think to look for her.

After a while she stretched herself out and lay, chin on hands, face almost against the glass. On the bay a small steamboat drew a bright color line across her field of vision and wavering reflections of itself in the water. A few fireflies, braving the cooling September night, glimmered through the curtains of moss. A burst of girl laughter and a subdued masculine roar sounded toward the bay. As in response, a light flared out across the grass from an opened door in the cottage, cutting off the laughter.

The attic gave strange protesting sounds and there came a sudden scratching in the chimney. A raccoon, maybe. They said that last year a raccoon had nested in a chimney that was not used except as a vent for the gas fireplace in Dr. Eloise's living room. Perhaps she and her babies were coming back. The scratching stopped, and everything fell intensely quiet. Tolly began to feel the past pressing down around her. She welcomed it, for it kept the present away. In the past this cramped space had been an infirmary, with cots set up on the rough floor, and kerosene lamps for light. Every inch of space and all manner of makeshifts had been used in those struggling days. Crowding at Mather was still necessary because the enrollment was far larger than before, but now the Board of Health and the Fire Department had to pass on all the makeshifts.

Tolly shivered in the sharp moist breeze that blew in at cracks and crevices. One didn't have to open windows to ventilate the cottage. Stiffly she gathered herself up and tiptoed across to the trap door. She pulled it open — cree-eeak — held it and her breath for a minute, crept under it and let it down — cree-eak — once more. She poised on the stair and listened. No one had roused. She stole down and into her room once more.

She had carried the letter with her. Now she put it back into its envelope, and snapped it into the small, rubber-banded pile she had accumulated, so that it should be just another letter.

She undressed and put on her prettiest nightgown. She would not let her heart be squeezed with pain like this again. At once, this minute, she would start to forget. She had been eating Rich's candy slowly, and had half a pound of it left. With the candy and a novel from the library she lay down on the bed, pulled an afghan over her, punched her pillow into a comfortable shape, and adjusted her bed lamp. She read and nibbled, while Miss Long's quick step clicked up the stair, paused, went on; till all sound had faded except the small tappings and rappings of the wind, fidgeting with something loose.

At last Tolly got up and knelt at the window, low like hers at home. She crossed her arms on the sill and rested her cheek on them. The moon flooded the bay with light, and there was no one but the moon and Tolly.

She heard a faraway bell that was audible only when the wind was right. Two o'clock. She crept back to bed and started again at the first of the novel. She could not make herself eat another chocolate. They were all soft centers. The few times Sojer had been able to buy her candy, he had chosen what she likel best, chocolate-dipped nuts, English toffee, pecan roll. It took time to learn what other people liked. She wasn't yet sure about Sojer's preferences.

She woke next morning, the light hot above her head, the book open on her stomach.

Gabe was waiting for her after breakfast. "Morning, Miss Tolly. You have time to kind of look over this paper of mine?"

With his solemn light eyes and the absurd wrinkles in his childish forehead he was like a dog, pleading for attention. He could get deep into her feelings if she would let him. And would it not take a miracle to make anything out of him?

Nearby Rosabelle was watchfully loitering, and Tolly beckoned to her. "Why don't you two join forces?" she asked crisply. "Gabe, Rosabelle has had several years of English at Mather and she speaks and writes well. Why not ask her to take a look at your paper?"

After a reproachful look at Tolly, Gabe turned politely to the other girl. "You mind, Rosabelle? Got time befo' this first class?"

And that evening Tolly deliberately tried to interest herself in a youth from the Marine Base at Parris Island. Anything would be better, she thought, than this cold numbness that held her.

Several trainees from the Base were attending night school three evenings a week at Mather, trying to make up high school credits toward their diplomas. It was too bad that they did not come in uniform, Tolly thought, but even without that advantage Claude Avery was personable, a clear-eyed, cocky, friendly boy, light on his feet and quick with his manners.

As if he had sensed a change in her attitude, he waited respectfully at her desk after class. "Miss Tolliver, will you excuse it if I seem to speak out of turn?"

"Go ahead, Claude," she said coolly. Already she knew it was no use trying to forget Sojer by playing round with a boy like Claude.

"Would you — would you care for a stroll in the

moonlight?" he asked, reddening through the pale brown of his cheeks.

He had temporarily lost some of his assurance, and she replied accordingly. "I'm a teacher, Claude. I doubt if Dr. Andrews would approve. But thank you," she added.

Rosabelle Gibbs had been waiting in the hall, looking curiously at the two of them. As Claude went out, murmuring something unintelligible, Rosabelle came in and stood hesitantly before the desk.

"Sit down, Rosabelle. Something on your mind?"

"I was wondering if that was another boy you'd like me to take over. He's as cute as Gabe, though nothing like him."

"Take him if you want to," Tolly said wearily. "But he would never worry me as Gabe would. I doubt if he has any ambition but to have a good time." Tolly's eyes sharpened as she looked at the pretty face before her. "That reminds me, Rosabelle — I never have found out what you're aiming at. Teaching? Secretarial work?"

Rosabelle's lips tightened before she answered. "I would have liked to be a teacher — But now I'm aiming at the sure thing. And the surest thing I know is cosmetology."

"But Rosabelle! Persons with the equipment you have, and the desire to teach — oh, I don't think anything should stop them."

"That's what my sister thought," Rosabelle answered somberly. "She is ten years older than I, and I always — well, worshiped her. She had everything: looks, sweetness, and one of those minds that's keen and deep, too. Gosh, but that girl worked hard. Got her college diploma, and what else? A job as a waitress. I don't want to stick my neck out as Zell did. Cosmetology is a good honest profession, and you can make money in it —"

"But Rosabelle!" Tolly repeated. "That was ten years ago. Things have changed, they really have. Surely you've heard the facts and figures: good jobs open to us with no one qualified to fill them — or else with the downright determination to — well, as you put it, stick their necks out and compete. Even my father says the time has come when we must assert ourselves. Quietly. Even gently. But take our legal place, and take our place in other ways as soon as we are fitted. He's been working at Negro registration for voting, himself."

"And then there are the sit-ins and the Freedom Rides," Rosabelle said. "And you know that little Jenniedeane Crowley? Did you hear about her protest?"

Well, if Rosabelle wanted to change the subject, Tolly wouldn't argue with her. "Protest? That mouse with the dimple?"

Rosabelle nodded. "Hers wasn't a sit-in. It was a kneel-in."

"A kneel-in? How do you mean?"

"She went to a white church in her home town."

"What on earth did she do? You'd think she'd cry if anyone poked a finger at her."

"Oh, nobody offered to touch her. An usher looked down his nose at her and said, 'Young woman, have you made a mistake?' She says she shook her head and went on into the nearest pew. No one did anything but look shocked and leave a big space around her. Next Sunday she went to another white church. Same deal. She says she can't see that it did a speck of good and she lost five pounds."

"They do say the protests have to be worked out carefully, and with enough people to make an impression," Tolly agreed.

"Well, I can't see why I should deliberately give myself an extra load of work and worry and danger," Rosabelle said decisively. "There's grief enough in just being born colored."

16

THAT NIGHT Tolly did not try nibbling chocolates any more, nor reading the novel. She had no idea what the novel was about, anyway. It had been a trivial way to try to heal a wound that went too deep. She did try to keep her mind away from Sojer. Dead? No! she still declared to herself. But — intentionally disappearing? That would mean — wouldn't it? — that he was giving up hope.

It had been a tragic experience for Sojer, his trying to cheat his way to graduation. It had been much harder for him than for her. But she could not live her life with someone who gave way to temptation, could she?

Determinedly she focused her thoughts on Rosabelle and Rosabelle's adored big sister. Rosabelle had spoken of her in the past tense —

She lay on her side, cheek on folded hands, and watched the moon rise and gild the water in a crinkled path. She watched it climb high and pour out a white radiance. She slept heavily, but woke at dawn and saw the sun come up in splendor. The Power and the Glory.

After breakfast she approached Dr. Eloise and asked

if the women at the Sales House could use a little extra help.

"Every bit of help is a tonic," said Dr. Eloise, her own special smile brightening. "Those are overworked women. Think how many boxes come in from all over the country! And goodness knows how we'd make ends meet if they didn't come. Those used clothes and miscellaneous articles take care of at least a fourth of our expenses. But you know all that."

Tolly did know, in a general way, the value of the Sales Houses, both here and formerly at Old Penn. They did a double service, letting the poorest of the people buy good clothing and house linens for the dimes and quarters which were all they had, allowing children to attend school who could not otherwise have gone in the damp chill of winter. Some of the good garments and articles stocked a thrift store for students who were scraping along on the most meager allowances.

"But Tolly, my dear," Dr. Andrews put in, "are you well? You look as if you had been burning the candle at both ends."

"I'm perfectly okay," Tolly assured her.

It was queer, she thought, that her eyes should feel as if she had been crying for hours, strained and gritty. She had not wept a tear last night.

She went over to the Sales House after her classes that afternoon and offered her services. With windows and doors open the women were still flushed and moist with heat and exercise. The staff member who had charge of the shipments was in the storeroom in the next building, wrestling to open well-packed and securely fastened boxes, while two workers were waiting on customers in the store. Tolly went at the prying open of boxes. As usual, they were varied. Here was one with good ordinary clothes, some slightly out of style, some faded, others attractive and new looking, but all clean and wearable. Here was one that contained a single garment, a monstrous fur coat. "Tk, tk!" said Miss Dell, shaking her head, when Tolly with an amused grimace held it out at arm's length. "We get it cold here, but not that cold."

"Maybe you'd better see if they are needing an extra hand in the store," she suggested a little later, dropping down on an especially difficult box and fanning herself vigorously.

Tolly ran over to the door and watched for a minute. A young mother and an old man were the only customers, the girl with a baby sitting astride her hip and staring with solemn amazement at the array of goods. Mrs. Adams was displaying overalls, shirts, sleepers in toddler size, and the mother was giggling her satisfaction at their sturdy prettiness and low price. When she had gathered a stack of needed things, she went to the desk to pay. Untying a big handkerchief, she carefully counted and recounted its coins. Soon she was on her way out, bundle on right hip and baby on left, her face one large smile.

"Here's a box that would go to the student store," Miss Dell told her when she returned, "good undies, slips, nighties —"

"May I carry them over for you?" Tolly offered. "It would give me just time to wash up for dinner."

She felt a little glow of satisfaction as she carried the awkward box across the highway that cut the campus, and down to the old building that housed the infirmary downstairs and student store upstairs. It was just beyond Mather Cottage and was the other of the remaining original buildings.

It was good to be helping someone, and this gave her just the right degree of participation: sympathetic, but remaining outside.

She had been too overwrought to notice that autumn was upon them. Lilies were still in bloom, and marigolds and other flowers, but the crape myrtle bushes marching the length of the walk from the entrance gate to the gymnasium had turned color and were like a row of bonfires lighting the way.

Autumn flowed on, and now Tolly was finding it full enough so that unhappy thoughts were pushed below the surface. She had an occasional letter from Langston, one almost every week from Rich. Ellen's were too few, and when they came they were bubbling over with the good times she was having, so many dates and festivities that Tolly wondered how she could chink in any minutes for study. Papa came now and then to Mather, often because registration matters brought him from St. Helena.

Rosabelle continued to coach Gabe and occasionally Melom, though she could help him only in idiom and pronunciation. He read almost every book in the Mather library, and over in the space above the Sales House storeroom, converted into a dormitory for the out-of-town boys, he studied until the small hours.

"But I do not wish to write a term paper on this subject," he told Tolly. "I mean to be a chief among my people, or one of the officials they now have instead of chiefs. What purpose will it serve for me to know the life of a man who wrote poetry a hundred years ago? I can not so waste my time."

He was walking with Tolly to the Sales House on a November day. The weather was still mild, with flowers blooming, but variegated leaves from the gum trees were drifting in the light wind.

"Let's peek in and see what they are doing in the store," Tolly said. "They may need me there, the way things look."

With colder weather ahead, people were flocking in greater numbers to the Sales House. Several pickup trucks, of varied ages and stages, waited outside, and the place was filled. Tolly went to work at once, and Melom stood back by the door to watch and listen. Tolly wondered whether he was thinking of the differences between his fellow tribesmen and these American Negroes.

It was when most of the customers had been served, or had found nothing to meet their needs, that an anxious-looking family hurried in. They had come from Coosaw Island. It was a far piece, as the man said, and they had trouble on the way. Coosaw was one island which still had neither bridge nor causeway. This family had crossed in the dugout canoe which was kept tied on one shore or the other, and then had borrowed a friend's mule and wagon. The old harness had broken twice, so that the man and the boys had had to stop and wire it together again. But they were purely desperate for clothes for thisyere gal-chile. No'm, she wasn't none of their-own: she was a motherless, a drift.

All attention turned to the child, probably ten years old. Eyes frightened, she shuffled along in men's shoes which her feet seemed barely able to lift, her ragged dress hanging limp below her knobby knees. She was curved sidewise under the weight of a solemn yearling who clutched her with tiny claws and nuzzled into her thin neck when anyone looked at him.

Mrs. Adams said, "Oh, thanks be to the white folks up North for the things they send! Look what a pretty dress for the little girl! And a slip to go with it — and socks and shoes — and I do believe this warm coat is the right size, too."

Tolly held the dress up against the drift, whose mouth twisted alarmingly as she gazed down at bright plaid and red binding. "Oh, little girl, don't you like it?" Tolly cried.

The child lifted wet eyes. "Fo' me?"

Tolly patted her with fingers that tried not to flinch from the grit and grime of the old dress. Eyes wide with entreaty, the girl held out the baby. Through his top garment could be seen another, and through its rags patches of brown skin. As for his knees, fingers, ears, Tolly wondered how they could have gathered so much grime in a year of living.

"Let's see," Mrs. Adams debated, "have you seen anything his size, Miss Phelps? If only those nice folks will hurry along some children's clothes —" With Miss Phelps and Tolly searching the piles on the many tables and the well-filled racks, they finally rooted out a pair of sturdy coveralls in toddler's size, a ship appliquéd on each knee.

The little girl had deposited the baby on the floor, but he scuttled to her at once, gripped her dress with one hand and thrust the other into his mouth, his eyes warning away all comers. She had slipped tiny feet out of the brogans and with shaking hands was pulling on the red socks.

"Oh," Tolly gasped, "oughtn't she to be washed first?"

The woman who had brought her was watching delightedly. "Tha's right, 'Melia. Oncet we gets home you tek you a good bath in the draw, so not to spile yo' good clothes. — Ma'am, yo' got any kind of dress fo' me? And shirt and overhalls fo' my man and them boys? And we got mo' chillen at home that would fit most any clothes you got —"

Her talk was more like the old Gullah than anything Tolly had lately heard, doubtless because Coosaw was so isolated.

Since the socks were on, Amelia put on the new brown oxfords. She extended them before her to adore them, while the baby stretched out a hand and tugged at a brown shoelace.

They were all startled when the woman, clasping a gay dress, burst into a rapturous shout. "Oh, Lawd, you good to usn this day. We t'anksful, t'anksful, t'anksful! Like the Good Book say, You clothe the naked and be father to the motherless. We t'anks You for the folks that send the clothes. They cain' help being white. Lawd, take them to Heaven just as if they was black like us! Glory hallelujah!"

Now she was not only singing and dancing, but "shouting," the shout being one of the old worship patterns. Miss Dell came over from the storage room, and the other customers stood watching, some echoing her praises, some tapping their feet in time to the music, while a few of the white people among them watched with amusement sometimes tinged with disgust, as if they were witnessing a questionable show.

"Amen!" said Mrs. Adams, deftly seizing the first interval, when the woman paused to get her breath and wipe her face on her sleeve. "Now I'll figure just how much these will cost. How much have you to invest, my friend?"

The woman named a small sum, evidently known

through many countings. "Good! A little will be left over," Mrs. Adams congratulated her.

"Ma'am, could we get'm —" the man nodded toward the little girl, still stroking the rich shine of the oxfords — "a pair of them beads? E pure raven fo' pretties."

"I'm sure you could," Mrs. Adams answered. "Tell us about her. A motherless, you said?"

Yes, a motherless. She had lost her parents and all her brothers and sisters except Ichabod. It was about a year earlier, when they had built a fire on the dirt floor of their ractify old cabin because the chimney had fallen. A wind had set fire to the wall when they were all asleep. This 'Melia had wakened just in time to lug Ichabod to safety, burning herself badly around the legs. They two, the only survivors, had come to live with this Unc' Jim and Sis' Noma and their twelve head of chillen. 'Melia had come to them with only the clothes on her back, the underclothes she slept in, Ichabod likewise. 'Melia was mighty handy. Looked like nobody else could master that little Ichabod.

"I wonder if I couldn't keep Ichabod awhile. We never had children."

Mrs. Adams's smooth brown face yearned toward the little fellow as she spoke. At once he wriggled, sitting, to his strong protector, round eyes defiant, and gripped her leg so tightly that she staggered to keep from falling on him.

"Yo' sho' welcome to'm. E a right likely lil boy, but boy chillen is one thing we ain't short of." Unc' Jim lowered his voice and gestured toward Amelia. "Better us act like nothing special. That lil gal —"

But Amelia's attention had been caught, and she gazed openmouthed from one to the other, then laid down the beads and darted to Ichabod.

Tolly felt a surge of pity. It would be far better for Ichabod if Mrs. Adams were to take him. It would probably be better for Amelia. But the separation was something Tolly did not want to see. Muttering an excuse, she turned and fled back to the cottage, entirely forgetting the waiting Melom.

That was Friday, and the next day the Tollivers drove up in the plum-colored car, to take Tolly home for the week end. She told them of the praise-meeting in the Sales House.

"But it will just about break that Amelia's heart," she said soberly. "She doesn't know when she's well off. Her skinny little body was bowed over already from lugging that heavy baby."

" 'Melia has involved herself." Mr. Tolliver spoke solemnly, but he pursed his lips over a smile. The smile did not last. He soon lapsed into the troubled silence that Tolly had often noticed of late.

"Papa, are you worried about something? Are you worried about Ellen? I know she isn't writing much, but then, she never did."

"It isn't so much Ellen, though I'm not quite easy about the child. But your old papa is no fighter, Tolly. I don't like setting folks edgewise. I've tried to obey the

Good Book where it says to be at peace with all men. Some of them get powerful mad when anyone, white or black, tries to make it possible for the Negro to vote. These days I don't feel as if I were living at peace with all men."

"Doesn't the Bible stick in something else, 'as far as in me lies'?" Dabney spoke up pertly from one of the puzzles he usually carried with him. "Me, I don't believe it in me lies to peacefully let those white men break the law. Law says we've got the vote."

His father neither reproved him nor laughed at him, but sighed deeply. "White lady near Yemassee, she phoned me this morning, and requested that I come to a council meeting tomorrow afternoon. To try to make clear the matter of the vote and the registration of Negroes. Goes against the grain for me to stand up and tell the white folks —"

"Well, then!" Tolly ejaculated.

"But now integration is the law of the land. And we are citizens," her father went on slowly. "Perhaps it is our duty to insist that the law be obeyed. Insist quietly, without violence. What is far harder, without hate. So —" He straightened sagging shoulders, tacked a smile on tight lips.

"Papa, let me go with you," Tolly said on impulse.

"Looks like I got no call to drag you into it, Tolly baby —"

But next afternoon she set out with him for Yemasee. In the clear November morning the marshes were tawny gold and brown, and every shining inlet held feeding cranes and avocets. Papa grew more and more somber and nervous. Once he patted the steering wheel with the gesture he used to make a point in a sermon. The horn blatted unexpectedly and he and Tolly jumped.

"But look, daughter — yonder is our meeting place, one of the prettiest country churches anywhere around."

It was beautiful, its spires and shining white columns pointing serenely upward. Yet as Papa eased the plum-colored car into the parking area, Tolly longed almost uncontrollably to run away, back to the haven of St. Helena.

People were loitering around the entrance, and as the two Tollivers stepped out of the car, all eyes seemed jerked toward them as if by an unheard signal. After the first instant, Tolly determinedly avoided those eyes. Stumbling along beside her father, she stared blindly ahead. Papa probably felt the same reluctance, for there was relief in his tone when he said, "Ah, Mrs. Brokaw."

A small, gentle-looking woman had appeared in the doorway, and now approached them, hand outstretched. "I'm so glad you could come, Mr. Tolliver. And this is your daughter? Good afternoon, Miss Tolliver. Will you come with me? It is time for the meeting to begin."

They followed her in, and down toward the front of the church.

"There is room for us here, with the committee," Mrs. Brokaw said. "I'll introduce you later. Our audience should be coming in," she added.

No one was coming in. The only persons in the church — the serene white church — were the committee, partly filling a few pews at the front, and Tolly, and Mr. Tolliver and the moderator. He sat on the platform, trying not to look uncomfortable, Tolly thought.

Sitting down, Mrs. Brokaw bowed her head on the pew before her and remained a long moment silent.

That is her usual way, Tolly thought, and now she needs to pray, because she is frightened. And so am I. And so is Papa. His hands are clenched and I can hear his roughened breath. And Papa ought not to have to feel this way for anyone.

"Will someone be so good as to go and tell the people outside that we are ready to start the meeting?" the man on the platform suggested.

At first no one stirred. The presiding officer moved one foot forward, placed the other beside it, drew them both back, made signals to the heavy-set man at the end of one of the pews. This man leaned forward and looked hopefully at the one on the farthest seat. He apparently tried to catch the other man's eye, failed, sighed, pulled himself to his feet. Running a forefinger around under his collar as if it were choking him, he went up the aisle to the door, shoes squeaking unevenly.

In the stillness of the church, outside noises were audible, though not words. There was no mistaking the tones, some derisive, some angry.

The tone of the messenger was also clearly understandable. First it simply announced, with a casualness that rang hollow. Then it grew mildly argumentative. Abruptly it was cut off, and scattered laughter, a few boos, and fewer remonstrances filled the intermission.

While some of the committee craned their necks to see what was happening, and others sat looking woodenly ahead, the emissary strode back. His stride was no longer reluctantly irregular, but angrily decisive. With a large white handkerchief he was mopping his face, thoroughly spattered by a ripe tomato.

The presiding officer was now standing glued to the floor behind the reading desk, his face turning scarlet under his tumble of silvery hair. He was swallowing visibly, and moistening his lips in order to speak.

"Since we have no one to whom we can make a report, let us sing a hymn," he said.

The small Mrs. Brokaw, in a surprisingly large voice, began: "Blest be the tie that binds / Our hearts in Christian love," and the committee one by one joined in the singing. Tolly thought she had never before sung more than two verses of the hymn. The final one came out clearly, with more volume than any of the rest.

The presiding officer raised a commanding hand and repeated the old Mizpah benediction, and by the time the committee and the Tollivers had silently left the auditorium, the loiterers outdoors had quieted, and let them through without trying to stop them.

"Won't some of you come to my house for a cup of tea?" Mrs. Brokaw's lips smiled but there was pain in her eyes. "You, especially, Mr. Tolliver, and Miss Tolliver, before your ride home."

"Thank you, gracious lady," Mr. Tolliver gently refused. "You have had more than enough of us for one day."

As they both responded with little bows and murmurs to other members of the committee, and went on to their car, acutely conscious of the critical glances that followed them, Tolly was smoldering with resentment. Yes, she was thinking, you committee members have had an unpleasant hour, but think how many hundreds of unpleasant hours Papa has gone through —

For a while they rode in complete silence, staring ahead. "Too still," said Papa after a while. "How about raising a spiritual, daughter?"

"I don't feel religious." Tolly's voice was edged with pain and anger. "Shall we sing 'Blest be the tie that binds'?" Or 'How sure a foundation'? What kind of shelter does God give us, anyhow?"

"Ever I think of our poet of the marshes," her father said, without rebuke in his voice. "How does he put it? 'As the marsh hen secretly builds on the watery sod, Behold, I will build me my nest on the goodness of God.' It's the truth, daughter. And this wasn't so bad. They've been known to kill a man — though not here — for what I have been doing. Let's forget it." Humming tentatively for a moment, he cleared his throat and began, "Were you there when they crucified my Lord?"

Papa was no singer, and Tolly was soon forced to join in and lead his vigorous off-key voice nearer the right course. Next he asked for an older, simpler song from the harsh days when slaves often found their only comfort in their religion: "It's me, it's me, it's me, O Lord, standing in the need of prayer."

Again Tolly joined in and overcame his discords with her strong, sweet harmonies. But those white folks stand in need of it far more than Papa does, she thought rebelliously.

Mr. Tolliver stopped at the "s'rimp factory" and purchased a fine lot of shrimps, fresh from the fishermen's boats. Mama had a specially tasty way of preparing them, each one looking like a butterfly and melting in the mouth.

She greeted them with some surprise, and Dabney came dashing out, book closed on finger. "You sure talked short, Papa. Why don't you do that way with your sermons? They're real good sermons," he hastened to add, "only a fellow does get the heeby-jeebies when he sits still so long."

"My speech was not short and sweet," Mr. Tolliver said, handing him the shrimps to carry in. "My speech *was not* — period. But we won't talk about it yet. For Jane Emmeline and myself the subject remains less than agreeable. Let us be happy together until time to go to church. And let us be thankful that it is granted to us to dwell in peace on St. Helena."

Mama outdid herself in preparing the shrimp, and to the menu she added a shortcake made with frozen strawberries from their own garden. She even consented when Dabney asked to turn on the TV during the meal, though the program was a comedy she had never enjoyed.

Tolly heard little of her father's sermon that night, but his voice calmed and strengthened her. Nor did she mind, as she usually did, the congregation's enthusiastic responses during the service. Thank goodness they were not a lot of lukewarm skim-milk Christians!

The four Tollivers were reasonably serene when they made ready for bed that night. You certainly couldn't allow such experiences to linger overnight. Every day you could count on something unhappy, something to sting and bruise. So you'd better not let anything rankle.

Tolly washed vigorously, for her ride had been a dusty one, and brushed her hair and tied it firmly in a scarf to keep the dampness of the air from spoiling its glossy smoothness. Her thoughts reached out to Sojer and she determinedly switched them to Rich. If she must think of boys at all, it would be better to think even of Langston.

Quietly she drifted off to sleep.

The sleep did not remain quiet. In her dreams an electric storm flashed its lightning across the dark, and voices called. Rousing a little, she knew that it was Dabney, calling, "Oh, Papa, Papa! Are you killed?" And presently Papa's voice, shaken and muffled, replying, "No, no, son, I'm definitely alive. Just missed the steps. Leg twisted under me —"

Shocked broad awake, Tolly went plunging down the stairs, out the front door, down the porch steps to the small group at their foot. Mama was trying to help Papa up, while Dabney dashed around them like an excited puppy. No one else was there.

But someone else had been there. The light that so weirdly jerked the group into full illumination and then dashed it into darkness again, that light did not come from the house. It came from an object in the midst of Mama's trampled petunias, whose broken blossoms filled the air with poignant sweetness.

That object was a burning cross.

17

TOLLY would never forget that night.

Papa pulled himself to his feet, making use of Mama's arm and Tolly's, the breath hissing between his teeth as if at a sharp hurt. With their help, he backed up to the steps and sat down, his legs stretched out before him.

"We got to — put that thing out," he said in a tone that tried to be normal. "The grass is pretty dry — might catch and spread."

They all looked at the flames, making no move toward them.

Burning crosses were common enough, set up by white-draped figures in hoods and masks in the yards of Negroes or of white people who sympathized with them. News of them had always brought sick horror to the Tollivers, all the more because the greatest symbol of goodness and love had been made the symbol of evil and hatred. And that one should ever come to St. Helena — that one should ever come to the Tollivers — it was unthinkable.

Almost at once neighbors began to appear, a few with

lanterns, more with flashlights. Some of the young men beat out the flames and tramped over the rest of the petunias to finish off the few sparks in the grass.

The rest gathered round the Tollivers, shivering in their nightclothes in the chill dark. Papa was answering their anxious questions. Half-waking, as Tolly had done, he had dimly thought that one of his children was walking in his sleep, and he had stumbled to the front door and out to the porch, from which direction the noises had seemed to come. There, to be sure, he had glimpsed a white-clad figure darting out through the gate. "Ellen!" he had called and, missing the steps, had plunged to the foot of them. Only then had the flaming-out of the cross thoroughly wakened him, together with the stabbing hurt in his twisted leg.

Someone had already telephoned Dr. Lincoln, and he and Mrs. Lincoln were soon there — Tolly wondering dimly whether the doctor ever really undressed and went to bed. While he examined Papa and taped his leg, Mrs. Lincoln was in the kitchen making coffee and the rest of the Tollivers were wrapping themselves in warm robes that covered them down to their slippered feet.

By that time the neighbors were filling the kitchen, and Tolly and Mama carried around cups of steaming coffee and plates of cookies from the jar Mama always kept filled. There was already a certain relaxing of tension. Some of the later comers had heard and seen the cars that had evidently brought the cross-burners, and had watched them out of sight, speeding silently toward Lady's Island and the great bridge. That evil presence was gone.

Dr. Lincoln would take Papa to Beaufort next morning for X rays, but his present opinion was that strained and twisted ligaments were probably the cause of the pain.

Tolly could almost imagine that this was some sort of social gathering, a work party, perhaps, though it was too subdued for that. It was more like a group giving and receiving comfort in time of sickness in the family. Everyone was trying not to be solemn, yet there was no fun left in them, and it seemed false and flippant when anyone attempted a joke. The menace of violence and hate was too close and ugly.

Tolly answered the telephone when it shrilled their ring. Dr. Andrews's voice sounded in her ear. "Tolly, we just heard. Are you all right?"

As she answered, Tolly could hear sibilant breathing that was not Dr. Andrews's; could hear someone's radio that had not been turned off though it was nearly one in the morning. Everyone on the island listened in, she thought, and this time she didn't mind. They were her friends.

"Well, if there's any way we can help, you have our number," Dr. Andrews's voice replied — a voice to lean on. "And, Tolly, with the Thanksgiving break coming up so soon, you stay over and help settle things down."

The two o'clock crowing of the roosters came, and

the neighbors gradually departed, swallowing their yawns.

"Let's all go to bed," Tolly said, "so we can face the day."

"A nap and a bath," Mama agreed, "and you can face anything."

"Better add a hair-do and powder on the nose." Tolly smiled faintly, thinking how much appearances meant to Mama.

Papa had to content himself with washing hands and face and stretching out on the couch where it was easier to manage his splinted leg. They all slept soundly until the ringing of the telephone wakened them.

Breakfast was hardly over when anxious, troubled, curious people began to appear. Later came the police officers from the town, asking questions that no one could answer. But it was next afternoon that an unfamiliar and jaunty sports car drove up to the Tolliver gate.

While Tolly stared, puzzled, Ellen leaped out and dashed through the gate and up the porch steps. She threw herself down before her father, who was sitting in the porch swing with his cumbersome leg extended before him, in the cast the Beaufort doctor had encased it in. Laughing and crying and kissing, Ellen paused only to wave airily at the dapper youth who carried her bag.

"This is Orbert, my classmate. Tolly knows him: — Langston's cousin. He brought me home the minute we got the news. Wasn't that wonderful of him? Papa, your leg will be okay in a little while, won't it? Is there anything to eat? Orbert and I are starved as well as sleepy."

Catching sight of Dabney, she scrambled to her feet and seized him. Holding him off to scan his face and then clutching him violently to her breast, she cried in a weeping voice, "My own little baby brother! The radio said you were all in danger of your life —"

With a muffled bellow Dabney wrenched free. "No such a thing! And listen at her: baby brother!"

It was while Ellen and Orbert were eating the food Mama had swiftly set out for them, that Stormy Waters came knocking at the back door. "I don't look fit," he apologized, when he saw Ellen, "but I had to come like I was, straight from work. Thought there might be something I could do."

Tolly watched with affectionate disapproval as Ellen's sleep-heavy eyes brightened and her slender shoulders straightened.

"Oooh, Stormy!" she cooed, "isn't that just sweet of you! Stormy, this is my classmate, Orbert. Orbert, Stormy Waters — isn't that the cutest name?"

"How dja do," Orbert commented.

"Pleased to meetcha," Stormy muttered, evidently without a shred of truth.

"Stormy —" Ellen's light voice veritably caressed the name — "you know what? First thing I thought was, Well, that big strong Stormy isn't far away. He'll help my darling family."

Tolly chucked in spite of herself. Yet something in

Ellen's expression puzzled her. It was coaxing, almost to the point of apology —

She was not entirely sorry that Ellen was still asleep next morning when another unexpected traveler drove up to the Tolliver door. Rich seemed fortified against Ellen's charm, but Tolly wondered if any boy could resist her. And in everything except boys, Tolly insisted even to herself, Ellen had real brains, besides being as sweet as she was silly.

Rich, too, had come straight from his Chicago law school as soon as he heard the news. He wanted to be sure there was nothing worse than reported.

"How did you hear it?" Dabney demanded.

Rich grinned at his eagerness. "Radio. TV. Newspapers."

"The famous Tollivers!" Dabney piped, strutting.

Ellen did come down before Rich took his departure, and she had never been prettier, nor her coaxing ways more nearly irresistible. Yet even her flirtatiousness seemed to grow thin and mechanical after a little and presently, when the four young people were on their way to reassure Aunt Emmeline, her feelings exploded, scattering her airy coquetry.

"It does make me so mad," she sputtered, looking like an infuriated kitten. "How could anyone, even white folks, want to be mean to such a darling family? Aren't they a darling family, Orbert, hm? Sweet old Papa, and Mama, and that little old scream of a Dabney — how could anyone hate them? You know what I'm going to do? I'm going on one of these Freedom Rides, and show just what I think of them."

"That's not what you're supposed to do on a Freedom Ride, Ellen," Rich corrected her indulgently. "First thing you have to do is to get hate out of yourself. Like Gandhi."

"Well, anyway," Ellen said lucidly, "you know what I mean. They're organizing a Ride in Nashville. Starts day after tomorrow. Don't tell Papa and Mama, but I'll be in it."

"Ellen baby, I'll have to tell Papa."

"I'll never forgive you if you do, sister. Never."

"I wouldn't mind going myself," Rich mused.

"Well, you can be sure of one thing," Tolly said flatly. "If Ellen goes, I go along to see she doesn't do something wild."

Orbert gritted his teeth, but his tone had a possessiveness that riled Tolly. "That will take the two of us, Tolly. Guess I can stand it once."

After a much shortened visit to Aunt Emmeline, the four took their proposal to Papa, who began by downright refusal.

"Papa," coaxed Ellen, "we'll only be standing up for our legal rights — quietly asserting our right to ride on the buses without being crowded into special seats, and to eat at the regular counters in the bus stations and all that. We do it without hate in ourselves. Like Gandhi. — And, Papa Tolliver, if you don't let me do this I'll go on a hunger strike. No fooling."

She stood with dimpled arms akimbo and eyes flashing, and Papa groaned. "Is that the way you talk to your papa, Ellen? Well, promise you'll all stick together — and try not to get arrested —"

Preparations went on with speed that left no time for second thoughts. First of all, Rich wired ahead to the Core group in Nashville. Tolly seized the telephone next and called Dr. Andrews. She had to go, she explained, to be sure that Ellen was looked after. "You know Ellen —" she said, her tone urgent. Yes, Dr. Andrews knew Ellen, and if Tolly thought she must do this thing, well, they would try to make do a little longer without her, if she was — detained.

By the time the girls had packed small bags and Mama had put up a hearty lunch — "and these boxes of crackers and cans of meat, just in case" — an answer had come from Nashville, telling the new Riders where to report on arrival.

The two cars and the four young people set out for their big adventure.

18

SERIOUS though the purpose of the Freedom Rides might be, this particular one started off gaily.

"But my little sister certainly needs a chaperone," Tolly said to Rich, watching Orbert's one-handed driving in the car ahead. Perhaps mindful of their presence, Ellen did not rest her head on his shoulder, but she sat near enough to do so.

"And that child is all teasing temptation," Tolly went on scolding. "I never did see her so — so delectable."

"Yeh, I know what you mean." Rich spoke like an uncle. "I'd want to spank my little sis. But she wouldn't be so dangerous, because she isn't half so pretty."

"Ellen's terrific, isn't she? Oh, if only she gets past these next years and anyway has her education!"

"For a sister, you're awfully keen about her."

"Always have been," Tolly said thoughtfully. "I was three when she was born, and Mama was so sick they never thought — Anyway, they put the little mite into my arms. Said she was my baby. I can remember — or maybe I only think I can — that she looked like a cherub. You've noticed how much prettier our babies are than new white ones."

"Never saw a new white one."

"They look sort of raw," Tolly said. "Ours are brown satin cupids." Brown satin angel, Sojer had often called Tolly. She shook her shoulders impatiently. "Look at that Orbert, scooping her over against him," she protested.

In a businesslike way Rich leaned on the horn and speeded up to overtake them, Ellen wriggling out of Orbert's clasp and pouting back at the chaperones. "This highway's out of bounds for smooching," Rich called, as businesslike as his horn.

The trip went on, with laughter and some song and the eating of the lunch they had brought from home and the hungry waiting for fair restaurants for their other meals, restaurants which would not wave them away with the sign White Only. Whenever they found one, they used their eating time for a briefing from Rich, who had taken part in several kinds of protests. They would be late at the meeting place in Nashville, and must have a good outline of what they were to do.

When they did reach Nashville after driving all night they were drowsy and tired, but their meeting with their Freedom Ride companions roused them.

Since it was the practice to have an equal number of white and Negro Riders, three more young white people had been recruited, making twelve in all, in addition to the observer, who did not take part in the action, but remained ready to get in touch with attorneys and bondsmen if they were needed.

The three latest Riders were already known to Tolly, Ellen, and Orbert. Sylvia Graham and Anthony Gallup were exchange students from Oberlin College. The third, with bright blue eyes and a shock of unconquerable pale hair, was affectionately called Brother Barry by his Fisk classmates. He was aiming at the ministry, and was appointed spokesman for this Ride, for it seemed to work out best for one to do all the talking that might be necessary.

A briskly efficient young insurance man asked quick, incisive questions of the newcomers, to be sure they understood the whole theory and practice of nonviolence. But he could see that they had the main principles well in mind. If there were enough time, though, they would set up situations that might arise and then act out ways of meeting them.

"It can get rough," he reminded them, looking thoughtfully at Ellen.

"But I ram my hands into my pockets —" this was Orbert — "even if a guy uses one of those electric shock sticks on me?"

"Worse: if he uses it on your girl."

"Grrr," said Orbert.

"You mustn't even feel hate," the leader persisted.

"I suppose the heart of it is," Rich put in thoughtfully, "we've got to have confidence that the universe is on the side of justice. As Martin Luther King says. And that the only effective motivation of these nonviolent protests is the love of God in the human heart."

"Brother Barry, here's another preacher," Orbert jeered.

"Harder than I thought," Tolly murmured, "but to keep an eye on Ellen —"

From this meeting, held in a Negro church, the four from St. Helena were guided to a host house which was ready for them, in a comfortable but all-Negro neighborhood. When they drove up Tolly was astonished to see two police dogs patrolling it inside a stout fence. "And the fellow cycling around is a guard," said the leader.

"I didn't dream everything was so carefully worked out," Tolly exclaimed. "People are always saying not to make a production of something. This is a production."

"We really need to register these protests, but we don't want to kill any more of you than is absolutely necessary." A deep seriousness lay behind the leader's banter.

"Ugh, I feel messy, up all night," Ellen said when they were ushered into the quietly pleasant house.

"You have time to refresh yourselves before dinner," their hostess said.

Their host was a lawyer, and the children grown and away. Tolly and Ellen were given the room of one of the daughters, and an adjoining bath, and the boys the bunks in the recreation room, with a shower handy.

"If you have clothes that need pressing," their hostess told them, "we have a cleaner in the next block who will get your things right back to you. It's included in the Freedom Ride," she added, laughing. "A package deal."

Baths, dinner and breakfast were as pleasant as at home, and Tolly said wryly to Ellen, "I feel like the condemned prisoner who has his choice of dinners before he goes to the electric chair. All these elaborate preparations make it more frightening."

"Now stop trying to scare me," Ellen said, stretching luxuriously after her bath. "You don't really think Orbert and Rich would let anything happen to us? Anthony and Brother Barry, either."

With her nightgown held over her head, Tolly stopped and stared. "Don't you listen to what they say, Ellen baby? We have put ourselves into a place where the boys can't help us, no matter what perfect knights they are. How can you smile like the cat who's eaten the canary?" she broke off. "You haven't heard a word I said."

"Mmmm — aaaah!" Ellen went into a vast yawn. "Tell me tomorrow, there's a nice sis. Right now I want to sleep — and sleep."

"I doubt if I get a single wink," Tolly grumbled. But she did, for the barking of the watchdogs wakened her. Creeping to the window she saw two men run to a car that idled at the curb. In another minute they were gone. Tolly shivered. Could they have done what they came to do? After another minute she heard the voice of their host, quieting the beasts. Evidently all was well. Tolly slept again.

The director of the Ride had bought their tickets to

a point beyond the state line, so that they would come under the laws for interstate travel. Without incident the twelve young people boarded the gleaming bus. Since it seemed the natural way, the sisters had been told to travel together as a pair; also Rich and Orbert, Anthony and Brother Barry. Just as well, the director said, to keep in segregated pairs, and attend only to the main business of the ride, to be served their meals without segregation, in the general dining room.

Tony and Brother Barry did sit companionably in front of Rich and Orbert, however, and the two white girl students, Sylvia and Barbara, one of the original group of riders, in front of the sisters. They tried to talk naturally, but their conversation was queerly constrained.

"My stomach feels — stiff," Tolly murmured.

"Common complaint," said Brother Barry. "Not knowing what may happen, or when — well, it tightens you up."

Tolly tried to feel a detached amusement as she watched some of the passengers. One old woman, getting on at a small town, stared blankly from Brother Barry and red-headed Anthony to Tolly and Ellen, who were talking to them. She looks as if we were committing an immorality, thought Tolly. Or as if Ellen and I carried deadly germs — like the Black Death. A white man gazed sternly from the window — and he looks as if he might be a good man, kind to his dogs. Two others made vicious remarks, which were meant to be heard, and were.

The noon meal stop was still in Tennessee. Tolly hadn't known whether she wanted the adventure to begin here or not, but it was with relief that she saw no warning sign over the bus eating place.

"So there is progress," Tolly said to Anthony and Brother Barry, at the same table. "Don't you think it would go on from here without any protests?"

"So slow we might not live to see it happen," Brother Barry said grimly. "And it was nonviolent action that got us this far."

The evening meal also passed without trouble, in an unsegregated lunchroom. And night should be restful, Tolly thought, stretching out in her chair when Rich had helped her lower it. But a tension was building up in her until she felt as if she might suddenly explode and shatter into a million pieces. Ellen also was tense. Once she gave a little scream and grabbed for her sister's hand without waking. It must be the fear of what morning might bring, Tolly thought, trying to get more comfortable, but cautiously, not to disturb Ellen.

Breakfast would be a test, for it was in a state less moderate than Tennessee. Tolly was almost glad when the hour came and the bus disgorged all its passengers at the terminal.

Here was the long familiar sign over the door: White Only. The other eating place was evidently around the corner, for the six white Freedom Riders started in that direction.

They believe they're acting unconcerned, Tolly

thought, her stomach contracting. Really, they walk as if they'd swallowed brooms. But so did Rich and Orbert. And so, she supposed, did she and Ellen. Try as she might, Tolly could not force herself to walk naturally.

For the first time in her life she pushed forward under that sign, White Only, as Rich held open the door. For the first time she sat at a counter where a few white customers stared incredulously at her.

"Did you see the police outside?" Rich asked conversationally.

Dumbly she shook her head.

A glaring waitress dashed toward the rear like a chicken crossing a busy road, but looking back over her shoulder with eyes that blazed with scorn and disgust. Two others drew away, folded idle arms across their chests, and stared scornfully at the Negro students.

"If looks could kill," Tolly wanted to say lightly to her companions, though she knew they were not supposed even to speak scoffingly. She could not speak at all, against that pressure of expectant hate.

Even Rich sounded unnatural when he said, "The stage manager is about to shift scenes."

Yes, this was like a carefully staged performance — up to a certain point. Tolly tried pretending that it was only stage fright that gripped her while the episode stretched and stretched like a movie film being shown in slow motion. A movie: the waitress mechanically serving some white customers but sparing venomous glances for the Negroes, the manager responding to the summons of the one waitress and striding across to a front door, head sunk between shoulders and jaws working agitatedly, and white customers sitting on the edge of their stools as if awaiting an explosion.

And then the police marched in, apparently later than they should have been.

"You love those guys, remember," Orbert muttered.

One of the officers stopped behind them. "Move on, you," he said, not very roughly.

"We merely wish to be served, sir" — even Rich's voice rasped with strain. "That is our legal right."

"Not in this state it ain't, boy. Now listen to me. We're here to protect you." He waved his club toward the mob gathering outside. "We sure wouldn't protect you if we didn't have to, but we have to. Now I'll tell you three times, and then you can darn well take the consequences."

He didn't wait for the first telling before he grasped Rich's arm with a powerful hand and jerked him from his stool. Another of the policemen enclosed Tolly's arm and Ellen's in a bruising grip and escorted them out of the place. Ahead of them Tolly could hear the first officer saying, "Move on out of here, y'all! Move on."

Countless times in her nineteen years Tolly had suffered cruel glances and ugly words, but never before had anyone laid rude hands upon her. She drew a deep, uneven breath, and bit her lip so sharply that she could taste the blood. Beyond the heavy, pear-shaped body of the officer, she could hear Ellen's soft gasps of shock and hurt. Hot rage scorched Tolly's face and neck at the sound.

Rich's half-smiling backward glance said, "Take it easy!"

Somewhat to Tolly's surprise, the Riders, though ungently handled, were "escorted" back to the bus and shoved aboard, rather than being thrown into jail. Tolly, who was ahead, whirled about as soon as she could right herself, and reached down to grasp Ellen's helplessly fluttering hands, so that she might be saved the bruising thrust against the metal steps. Ellen was stifling frightened sobs, her face that of a child expecting a reprimand and receiving a wound.

Orbert, some distance to the rear, looked at Ellen as if she were fine china being roughly handled. I'd like him for it, if he had any right, Tolly thought.

The bus had to wait till the white passengers finished breakfast and returned. Tolly, sitting hot and miserable, holding Ellen's hand, noticed again the variety of expressions. The one man still stared out of the window, while those who had mouthed the coarse epithets ostentatiously picked their teeth, and smirked mockingly at the hungry Riders.

Brother Barry pulled a paper sack from his pocket and passed it. "Who needs a breakfast?" he asked them. "This pure glucose goes straight to work to make you over new."

The last passengers straggled back and hoisted themselves up the steep steps while the driver honked a warning. The door clanged shut and the bus roared into motion.

"We lived through it, didn't we?" Ellen chirped. "Maybe that's the worst —"

Rich said, "Don't count on anything like that. I have a hunch."

"Hunch was right." Brother Barry leaned across the aisle and spoke low: "Notice the cars that have been meeting us? And the funny little honks the bus driver gives? Well, now watch."

They watched. Several cars made U-turns and sped in the direction the bus was taking.

"Oh-oh," Rich said. "Roadblock.

Almost at the same moment, with a long screech of brakes, the bus came to a sudden stop that banged the passengers against seats in front of them.

"A — a mob!" Ellen whispered.

Incredulous, Tolly saw that the mob was made up partly of well-dressed white men, in slacks and sport coats, their gleaming pastel cars parked at the side of the highway. Many carried large paper bags. "Iron bars and lead pipe in those sacks," said Rich.

Hardly had the bus stopped when the mob engulfed it, battering windows and metal sides, yelling, shouting words that made Tolly's insides swell and shrivel. It was as if they had slipped off their civilization like topcoats.

Senselessly she was telling herself, "I am confident that the universe is on the side of justice —"

"Duck!" Rich ordered.

As they ducked, the window beside them broke with a crash and a tinkle. At once the vehicle filled with acrid smoke that set everyone coughing and strangling.

"Down on — floor!" Brother Barry wheezed. "Better air —"

"Gosh — got to get out —" Orbert gasped. "Rather risk it than be roasted —"

"They wouldn't — burn the bus?" Tolly demanded of Rich, beside her on the floor.

"Man, wouldn't they! Ugly mob — no police —"

Orbert, bent double and clutching at his throat, was running toward the door. Squirming around to peer through steaming eyes, Tolly saw that it was held shut by the mob. She stared back at Ellen. "I can't — can't let her be —"

Now Brother Barry was flying up the aisle like a catapulted jacknife. His good, ugly face set grimly, his flaxen hair thrown back, he eyed the door as he ran. With no room nor time to maneuver, he hurled himself at it, his substantial weight multiplied by his speed.

The door gave way so suddenly that he and Orbert flew out into the howling pack. Taken by surprise, it gave ground. The bus poured forth a breathless, coughing, sneezing human avalanche, eyes flowing and cuts from splintered glass streaming red. The old woman glared her righteous indignation, and the evil-tongued men were momentarily silent.

Then a wild cheer rose from the fringe of the mob, and

174

one man jumped up and down, whistling raucously and waving a triumphant bludgeon toward the bus. With a loud crackle and hiss it burst into flame.

Persecuted and persecutors alike scattered to get out of reach of the explosions likely to come when the heat reached the gasoline. The mob were too busy protecting themselves to lay about them with their weapons. Perhaps, too, the affair had gone further than intended.

Before the Freedom Riders could be more savagely assaulted another bus, almost empty, drew to a halt as near as was safe, and its driver came loping up to confer with the first driver. Tolly found herself with her companions running back toward the second bus and finding seats there. By this time the vituperative white passengers had regained the power of speech and were using it without moderation, staring with ugly grins at the Riders.

"But this really will be all?" Ellen implored Orbert with soft eyes reddened by tear-gas fumes.

She looks to that lightweight boy for comfort instead of to me, Tolly thought with a pang.

"No, this mob isn't through," Rich said soberly. "Look. Their cars are racing for the next town. Bad town, too."

He was right. When they pulled in to the next station the crowd surged upon them again.

"Must we get off here?" Tolly asked. "Haven't we risked enough for this time?"

"No, girl, we haven't," Rich said gently. "And back in Nashville they said another big load of Riders is to join us here. Spot news, that may make. Compel the attention of the world."

Tolly stood glued to the bus steps. She had turned to jelly, and her feet could not move down, especially with Ellen having to follow her.

For the mob had swung into action, and no police were there. Never before had Tolly heard the sound of blows crashing on human flesh. It turned her sick. In that poised instant, her eyes were pulled ahead to the passengers from the other bus and to one young man there. Tall and skeleton-thin, he swung his left arm as if he were about to fling it from him.

As if drawn by Tolly's eyes, he turned his head a little. Tolly could see only the set of jaw and slant of ear — Before she could focus her inflamed eyes again, a terrific blow had fallen on that turned head. As if struck by an electric current, the thin figure jerked to a stop and its balled fists came up purposefully.

Then the fists unclenched, the arms dropped, the young man stood as if passively awaiting the next blow. When it came, he crumpled sidewise into the crowd.

It was not Sojer. Of course it was not Sojer. Yet, forgetting her own danger, forgetting even Ellen's, she struggled to push toward him. No use. She was seized and beaten this way and that. Someone thrust a lighted cigarette against her neck and when she whirled around a stinging slap on the face sent her staggering. Shoving, kicking, raining blows on defenseless bodies, the mob surged to and fro.

"Protect — your face, Ellen!" she croaked, remembering what Rich and the leader at Nashville had told them. "Arms up — like this —"

Brother Barry, for all his athlete's body, could not stand against the manifold violence. He was fighting his way toward Ellen, as if meaning to shield her, when Tolly saw an iron pipe poised over his blond head from behind, the face of its wielder crimson with rage, teeth bared.

"Barry!" Tolly screamed, just as the blow fell.

Like the other young man, Barry crumpled and went down among the trampling feet. With sick horror, Tolly saw a heavy boot lifted in a deliberate kick at his head as he lay there.

Negro students also had fallen, and some lay helplessly groaning. A whistle tore through the hard-breathing, yelling, scuffling commotion, and the mob began to melt before the oncoming and strangely late police. Tolly's eyes probed ahead for any glimpse of the tall youth with the swinging arm. He was nowhere to be seen.

Almost simultaneously with the police came an ambulance, siren wailing. Tolly saw at once that it was a white people's ambulance, probably sent to attend any injured white passengers from the burned bus. She beckoned violently, pointing to Brother Barry, who lay face upward and eyes closed, head in a thickening red pool.

The ambulance men stared at him, conferred with the bus drivers, and then shook brusque heads. "We don't take no fool Freedom Riders," they said, and clanged away.

And now the police were striding through the throng. "Move on! Move on, you!" they commanded, shoving almost as roughly as had the mob.

"We needn't move on, sir," Rich said as evenly as his pumping lungs would permit. "Don't move on, folks."

"Then you're under arrest." The officer swung a fist against Rich's jaw.

"What charge, sir?" asked Rich, when he had spat out the blood.

"Breach of the peace, smart boy."

Again the bruising hand on Tolly's arm, dragging her away. Desperately she looked back at Brother Barry, now lying in an open space, with rain beginning to fall upon his still, gray-white face. "That man — he's terribly hurt!" she cried.

"His own blasted fault," the policeman snarled, and tightened his grasp.

19

FOR MONTHS now newspapers, radio, common talk had
been filled with the hundreds of Negroes going to jail
in nonviolent protest. Not Negroes from the lower strata,
but ministers, teachers, and especially college students.
Martin Luther King had given them a clarion call:
They must crowd the jails to help gain their moral and
legal rights.

Jail had become a common idea to Tolly, an idea
tinged with doubting admiration for the forceful charac-
ter of people who would deliberately bring upon themselves such humiliation and danger. She had wondered
if Arna Bontemps, Fisk's noted author-librarian, had
felt any of her doubt when he called the sit-ins and Freedom Rides a Children's Crusade, because students were
the prime movers. Tolly had thought it resembled that
long-ago desperate venture in being unwise as well as
noble and heroic.

But now the word "jail" had a different shape and
taste. It was not just jail, but jail for Tolly and Ellen.

As a preliminary they were taken somewhere and
fingerprinted. "Like common criminals," Ellen pro-

tested when an officer rammed her small fingers down on the ink and then on the paper.

"Your own doings. Why you want to come down here and stir up a ruckus I'll never know," he growled. "We treat our niggers fine. They didn't have any complaints until the communists sicked you on to them to rouse them up."

"Sir," said Rich, "no communist has come near us."

His words seemed to bounce off the policeman's set face.

Their next experience was the ride to jail. "This is the paddy-wagon," Rich instructed them as the girls tried to fold themselves into themselves and avoid the grimy, ill-smelling seats and walls.

Jail was no pleasanter — damp, chill, and odorous. As the girls were hustled through the segregated women's wing, dark faces peered out at them, a drunken woman screeched at them.

"Don't look for any sympathy from these niggers," the officer snapped. "If anything, they hate you worse than the whites do."

He thrust the two into a cell, banged and locked the door, strode away.

Ellen stared at Tolly. "Us," she said ungrammatically, "Us — in jail. And, oh, Tolly! I can't sit on one of those unspeakable bunks. But I can't stand on this unspeakable floor." She broke into a weeping, shaking, quivering, no less intense for being almost silent.

Tolly's heart ached for her, but she spoke firmly,

drawing the girl into her arms. "Ellen, whose idea was this in the first place? None of us would be here if you hadn't insisted on coming yourself. Oh, I know it was your love for our folks, but there's truth in the old saying about making your bed and having to lie in it."

Her quiet steady voice had gradually relaxed Ellen's trembling body. Ellen quavered, "If only the boys were with us, I'd feel safer. If only Orbert—"

Tolly tried to laugh. "I never did hear of their putting men and women prisoners together, baby. We may not be here long," she went on. "We'd better make mental notes of the place, so we can give talks: Confessions of an Ex-Convict or something. Come, sit down on the edge of a bunk. We're washable: fast color, you know, guaranteed not to run."

They sat down, for their knees shook, their heads and bruised bodies ached. Now that the excitement had ebbed, the cigarette burn smarted angrily, and Tolly stuffed between it and her sweater the cleanest handkerchief she could find. Ellen crouched in the curve of Tolly's arm, leaned her head on Tolly's shoulder, closed her eyes. Tolly looked about her with an active curiosity. After all, she hoped to be a writer some day, and this was an experience she could use.

Cement floor and walls and iron-barred door that prevented privacy. Four bunks in pairs, one above another. A commode in one corner. A sort of sink, but without running water, only a bucket on the floor.

The door rattled. A Negro trusty was setting a tray on

a shelf below a slot in the bars. Tolly shrank back, remembering the officer's words about the hatred of the Negro prisoners.

"Don't be scared of me, Missy," he said gently. "I'd help you efn I could. I pick out the best-looking plates for you and the other little missy. I got gal chillen of my own at home."

Tolly's eyes filled with tears at the unexpected kindness, and she thanked him as she drew one tray and another through the slot. For a long minute she stared at the graceless pie tins balanced on their knees, and then she began to giggle.

"How you can laugh!" Ellen protested.

"Baby, remember how Papa used to put a bit of Mama's wonderful fried chicken on a fork and hold it to your stubborn little closed mouth and say, 'Tucka tucka tucka, tuck tuck too!' You were a little dickens about eating, and Papa and Mama took no stock in the notion of not urging a child."

"Mama's fried chicken! And look at this!" Ellen cried.

The tins were rusty and cold fat had congealed on the barbecued necks and wings. Beside them were a slab of sweet potato and a slice of grayish bread.

"Do you know how long it's been since we ate?" Tolly resolutely picked up a wing and nibbled. "All we've had since last night is Brother Barry's butterscotch — poor Barry! — and a chocolate bar I had in my bag. I guess when you're hungry enough you'll eat anything. And this could be worse. You better try it."

"With my hands as dirty as this?"

"Well, maybe we can get a little cleaner. Just maybe."

They soaked the one wafer of secondhand soap in a little water — soap could be disgusting! — and got more or less fresh water from the bucket. Vigorously they lathered their hands and shook them dry.

"Goodness, but that makes me feel better," Tolly exclaimed. "Hungrier, too."

Both ate every bit of the distasteful food, and their spirits lifted noticeably. They were in condition to tune in on the sounds that began to reach them from the men's quarters in the small jail. The Riders were singing.

They knew it was the Freedom Riders, both because of the songs and because Tolly recognized Rich's strong, rather tuneless voice. "Listen!" she said, "that's one of the best."

> *"We shall overcome! We shall overcome!*
> *We shall overcome some day!*
> *Deep in my heart I do believe*
> *We shall overcome some day!"*

There was power in the song, and faith. From that they went on to others, written purposely for the protests, and sung to hymn tunes that everyone knew. Soon Tolly's velvety contralto, with its considerable volume, joined with them, and Ellen's canary chirp fell into line. Other Riders down the women's corridors joined the singing, as did some of the other prisoners.

They sang themselves hoarse. Singing helped pass the

time — "and there were never so many minutes in an hour," Tolly said.

The trusty who had spoken kindly brought their supper, a sweet roll, a cup of watery coffee and a smile. Strange, Tolly thought, how beautiful a smile could be. The man's face was low of brow and had a jutting jaw, but his smile made the supper edible. It was like a little flame in the darkness or a glowing ember in the cold.

As he shoved in a tray he cautioned, "Take it careful, young Missy. Sometimes the bottoms of these trays is slippery. — Now how ever this got here?" He indicated a stump of pencil under the edge of the plate.

"I catch," said Tolly, and took her tray with both hands, one for holding, the other for feeling. A folded paper was stuck to the underside. With chewing gum, maybe — but Tolly mustn't be fussy.

When he had gone on, they pulled loose the papers from both trays.

On one Rich had penciled a few words: "Sit tight. Our observer will have made contact with the nearest Core man. He'll likely be here in the morning and see that there's a hearing. He'll likely get bail, too, for any who don't want to do a jail-in. A jail-in is effective. The world focuses on a group who choose to do time to register their convictions. This trusty is a good guy. Didn't do a thing but slice another man with a razor when he was drunk. He'll fetch us your notes somehow."

Ellen didn't share Orbert's note with her sister, but merely said that he advised their accepting bail.

The writing of replies had its difficulties, but none that could not be overcome. Since the girls had no paper, Tolly used the back of Rich's note, and Ellen tore off the blank paper at the bottom of Orbert's, stuffing the note itself down her neck. Lacking a good surface to rest the paper on, Tolly crouched in a lower berth with Ellen sitting on the edge to shield her from view, held the paper against the rough wall, and wrote with the stub of pencil.

"Written by guess and by golly," she said, holding it near her eyes to read it. " 'It may not be cricket, but we'll take bail. I can't have Ellen stay here any longer than necessary. She was always delicate.' That suit you okay, baby?"

Ellen smiled vaguely and reached for the pencil.

The trusty, when he came, winked and slid the two notes up his sleeve.

Tolly was thinking, I wonder if the Core man, when he comes, can find out for sure that the man I saw was not Sojer. She could not seem to put away the sight of Brother Barry's gray-white face and his fair bloodied hair, nor of the youth with the arm that swung like Sojer's. Again and again she saw them crumple under the savage rain of blows.

"What did Orbert have to offer?" she asked, trying to get her thoughts on another track.

"Nice things," Ellen cooed, her pinched face glowing.

"About our present situation?" Tolly prompted. "I'd give a bushel of gooey words for one mouthful of broiled steak — and a carload of them to be out of here."

"Oh —" Ellen smoothed out the folded paper. " 'We'll accept bail, naturally, honey. You bet your sweet life I'll jump at it like a trout at a worm. We'd be nuts not to. Haven't we done our bit? And when we get away —' oh, that's rather personal." She folded the note tight and thrust it back into its hiding place.

The boys started another sing that evening. It was a relief, for the minutes moved so slowly that Tolly could not believe they moved at all, and there was nothing to do. There was, of course, not a page of reading material in reach. They began to repeat poetry they had memorized, and Bible verses, and devoutly wished they had learned more of them.

So they joined more heartily than before in the singing, and Tolly almost missed Rich's improvisation when he sang, "Hold the fort, for Core is coming!"

They sang even after a jailer came stamping along the corridors, barking out commands. "A little more of this racket and some of you will get solitary. Button up your lips, you niggers."

Niggers. Why did that often-heard word always have the power to wound? It was like a harsh discord. It was like salt rubbed into a raw cut. It was like flung filth.

But since the boys went on singing, Tolly gulped down her resentment and sang too. This song was unfamiliar, but she soon caught on, and enjoyed the chuckle that ran through the words "I'll tell God how you treated me." That was how it had been in slavery days, Tolly thought, when for many a slave in his despair there was no one to tell except God.

It was not long before the jailer was shouting and swearing through the corridors again. "Don't say I didn't warn you. If you rather sing than sleep, okay. — They don't need no mattresses, boys. Take 'em away."

Guards came into the girls' cell, yanked the limp, stained mattresses from all four bunks and stamped out again.

"Well, it's something to get rid of those abominable things!" Tolly exclaimed. "I didn't want to mention it, but I'm sure there were — bedbugs. I'd rather lie on the springs."

Everyone sang awhile longer. In the pauses comments were shouted from both Negro and white wings. Some were brutal, but most took the other angle.

"Keep it up!" called one. "We're for you, only we ain't got the guts to do anything about it."

"Keep a stiff upper lip, Freedom Riders! And sing us some more."

At last the day's weariness took command, and a deep silence fell, broken only by the periodic pounding of guards' boots along the halls, and occasional drunken shouting from the cells.

Both girls turned from side to side on the bare steel of the bunks, trying vainly to ease the pressure on their sore flesh and bones. Even through handkerchief and sweaters, the iron punished Tolly's burn so that it throbbed heavily. Tolly would have said that she had measured the endless hours of the night by minutes. But she knew that she must have slept, for the look of things changed. The shadows of the cell bars, which had lain clear and black against floor and wall, were less sharp as morning light oozed in, and the same trusty was shoving in their breakfast.

Again there were notes from the boys. Again Ellen read Orbert's to herself, with a secret smile. Rich's said that he and Orbert would take bail, too, if offered. Orbert wanted to and Rich felt that he must see Tolly safely home. He would have other chances to protest.

Surprisingly soon they were haled before the court. One of the officers who had dragged them off to jail was there, staring at the students with a sneer. Tolly picked out a quietly well-dressed Negro with thick glasses as the attorney sent by Core.

Even here they were segregated, white prisoners, their attorneys and witnesses, on one side, and Negro on the other. Later Rich told Tolly that the Bibles on which they placed their hands when they took oath were segregated, too. "Of course. Think how shocking it would be if a white man swore on a colored Bible."

One of the first questions was how long the Freedom Riders had been given to obey the police order to disperse. "Fifteen seconds," a police officer snapped.

The Negro attorney looked significantly at the judge, who scowled unhappily and agreed that the time was inadequate. "Lieutenant, did I hear correctly? Fifteen seconds?"

The lieutenant reddened. "Fifteen minutes, your honor," he amended hastily, while the judge frowned at the subdued titter that greeted the words.

The questioning went on and on, and Tolly warmed with pride at the skill and courtesy of their attorney. The case was perfectly clear, and she waited expectantly for the verdict.

The uncomfortable-looking judge moistened his lips and spoke: "Guilty. Sixty days hard labor in jail."

20

Sixty days hard labor in jail.

Twenty-four endless hours in each day. Sixty slow minutes in every hour. Each minute nauseating with smells, hunger, bugs, roaches, and words more sickening than any of these.

He had actually rendered the sentence. While the room flickered dizzily before Tolly, Ellen, who had risen for the verdict as ordered, slithered down in a soft little heap on the floor. Fainting was a nice easy way of meeting an emergency, Tolly thought with impatient pity.

What would the bail be? the attorney asked the judge.

One thousand dollars apiece for the ten before him, the judge replied grimly.

Again the room darkened and teetered. Ten thousand dollars. How could they ever raise that sum? Tolly's eyes leaped to the attorney. With a wave of relief she saw that he was not taken aback by the size of the sum demanded, but was saying something about making contact at once with the bondsmen. They were lucky, he congratulated the Riders when they were outside the courtroom. This was Saturday and court convened again

Monday. They would have only two more nights in jail.

Only twice as long as the eternity they had just passed through. Tolly got a firm grip on Ellen for fear she would faint again.

At the same time, Tolly was hurriedly appealing to the attorney. Through the nightmare the image of the young man with the swinging arm had persisted. "These at the hearing today — they weren't the whole of the two Freedom Rides?" she asked.

"No, some landed in the hospital."

"Do you have all their names?" Her voice shook with excitement.

"Oh, yes, we're kept informed of all who embark on any of these nonviolent protests."

"Then in the other bus could there have been a young man named Pratt, S. J. Pratt?"

"I think not, but I'll make sure."

"Move on, y'all. Paddy-wagon's waiting."

The attorney rode to the jail with them, precariously balancing himself rather than sitting down. Tolly held her breath while he brought a typed list close to his thick glasses, and scanned it from top to bottom. The breath went out of her as he returned it to his pocket, shaking his head. "No S. J. Pratt."

In response to her companions' surprised lift of brows, Tolly threw out deprecatory hands. "Silly, wasn't it? One of the fellows that came in on that next Ride reminded me of Sojer. I didn't get a good look at him. It was just about the time Barry was so badly beaten —"

she shuddered — "They knocked him down, the one who looked like Sojer — looked like him from the back," she added as if reassuring herself.

Rich had been listening gravely. "How is Barry?" he asked the attorney. "And where?"

"They got him into the hospital, but I judge he had lain in the street for an hour before they did anything. They say there were two Negroes holding umbrellas over him. Raining."

"Probably lose their jobs for that," Rich said. "Think his case is serious?"

"Could hardly be otherwise under the circumstances. Barring infection, though, they think he'll pull through. Fifty stitches. Can't you see his picture, printed all over the world, 'Young white minister, Freedom Rider, beaten by racist mob'? And him peering out of yards and yards of bandage."

The guard had been listening scornfully. Now he snarled, "Cut the talk, y'all. This ain't no tea party."

Tolly spent the rest of the ride figuring hours and minutes again. As a would-be writer she tried to find words to fit the heavy, inching progress of those hours and the load of horror they could carry.

They did pass, more disgusting, aching, nauseous, frightening than she had been able to imagine them, and the Riders were at last released — "to be recalled for trial later," Rich reminded her.

And now it was release that seemed like a dream, and

their return to Nashville not as Freedom Riders but as mere quiet young people.

On the campus again, Tolly got permission to stay overnight in Ellen's room, and Rich in Orbert's. The girls' baths were their first luxurious enjoyment, though the lash of hot, soapy water on that cigarette burn made Tolly wince and call Ellen to look at it. It was angrily inflamed, Ellen said, as she dabbed it with merthiolate and crisscrossed it with adhesive bandages. Bed came next, as soon as they could half satisfy the girls who crowded in to hear their adventure. At last the door was shut, and Ellen's roommate temporarily stilled. In spite of being jammed two in a single bed, the girls richly relished the softness and cleanness under and around them, the freshness of the air, and the lovely quiet that was broken by nothing nearer than late cars on the highway.

Rich and Orbert joined them for breakfast, which was another luxury. "And we used to gripe about the meals here!" Tolly marveled, relishing a bite of rice cake with honey.

"We, too," Rich agreed. "Every student, everywhere, gripes about the food. It's one of the facts of life."

"Couldn't we go to the kitchen and buy a dozen of these sticky cinnamon rolls?" Tolly closed her eyes as she took the first luscious bite. "Mmmm. Could you get them into your pocket, Rich?"

"You want to pay the cleaner's bill, woman? But maybe they'd give us a paper bag."

The two were speeding back toward St. Helena after Tolly had asked Ellen a few searching questions, and had scrutinized her in the bright morning sunlight.

"I'm surprised you didn't take her temperature," Rich teased as they zoomed away.

"She didn't have any fever," Tolly said matter-of-factly. "Her pulse was as steady as mine."

Rich threw back his head and laughed. "You actually took her pulse!"

"I had to be ready to reassure Mama that little Ellen hadn't suffered permanent damage," she said defensively.

"Yeah, folks are like that. My mother will admit that I've got along on my own all these college years, but she still wants to know if I drink my quart of milk a day. She'll feel a lot better when she sees for herself that I'm all in one piece."

"But if it hadn't been for me you could have gone right back to law school. And I've hardly thanked you."

"It's Mother that'll be thanking you for letting her get a look at me. My folks aren't strong for the non-violent resistance. Like others who've had it better than the run of our people, they'd rather go slow, get us all educated, and so commanding respect instead of having to demand it."

"Right now I'm all in a muddle," Tolly admitted. "But when I think of Sojer I know one thing for sure, even if I have to hide it. I can't forgive the white folks for keeping us so ignorant that most of us aren't ready to compete."

"This Sojer — it's him I'm muddled about. You seem still to think a lot of the fellow."

"Not of him — about him." Tolly's eyes flashed. "How can I help thinking a lot about him? You don't put all that time and effort into a person's success and not think about him. But caring for him is something else again. I suppose you could say that I hate Sojourner Truth Pratt. Now let's talk of something else."

They talked of everything else. They talked of how bright the autumn color remained, even now, after Thanksgiving. "Thanksgiving! Heavens, what became of Thanksgiving?" Tolly exclaimed.

They talked of the Chinese tallow trees bordering stretches of woodland like bright little bonfires. The maples blazed in various flames of vermilion and yellow, and oaks smoldered deeply red.

Tolly took the wheel in the afternoon, so that Rich could doze and be ready to do the night driving. She drove until deep dusk, when they came to a drive-in which would serve them with hamburgers and coffee, so long as they would take the food away and not disgrace the place by stopping in front to eat.

Rich woke out of deep sleep when the car stopped, and had slid into the driver's seat when she brought back their order, precariously balanced. "My aunt's eyebrow!" he said, the words thickened by a yawn. "You shouldn't have let me sleep so long."

Tolly dozed, dreamed, wakened, slumbered again, through the long night, and this time it was Rich who drew up at a truck stop and brought out their breakfast. When they were on their way again, he broke the silence abruptly, as if with thoughts long stirring while Tolly slept.

"You resent the white people. But what about Mather? What about Old Penn? They, and most of our other schools, were started by white people. You can't lump them all, the way they lump all of us. — How is that Chinese proverb I once heard you mention? 'Better to light one candle —' What's the rest of it?"

"Oh, that. 'Better to light one candle than to curse the darkness.' The trouble is, you have to go into the dark to light that candle. Have to involve yourself."

"Yet you're anything but distant toward Ellen. Or the rest of your family. Or Aunt Emmeline. Makes you think of the man who prayed, 'God bless me and my wife, my son John and his wife —' "

" 'Us four and no more,' " Tolly completed the jingle, snapping the words off irritably. "Lucky we aren't in traffic. Your mind doesn't seem to be on your driving. Honestly, Rich, you don't like me much, do you?"

Instead of protesting, he answered slowly, almost sadly. "Like you? It isn't a matter of liking, Jane Emmeline Tolliver. Almost from the first time I laid eyes on you I've been fighting against loving you. Tolly, I don't want to love you. And I don't intend to. — And I'm getting over it."

"Well!" Tolly gasped, finding no words.

"My wife's got to have a heart as big as the world!" Rich was hoarse with passion. "And even if I should do something really wrong, she's got to be the kind that will keep on loving me. I could do anything, be anything, for a woman like that."

Tolly found a thread of voice. "Isn't it lucky, then, that I haven't let myself fall in love with you, Rich?"

For a while they rode in silence. Now and then Tolly let herself glance at his strong, definite profile, the planes of his lips clear-cut and flat in the best fashion of their race, the eyes so keen and steady under straight brows. She never had felt for him what she once had felt for Sojer. But — it would have grown. And now —

She sniffed and grabbed for her handkerchief.

"Don't!" Rich's voice was rough with pain. "I'm no gentleman, am I? But somehow I had to tell you."

"I suppose now you can go back to the girl in Chicago."

Rich shook his head. "She's an awfully nice girl. But I'll have to wait till I can forget you a little. Every time I look at anyone else your face comes between. Those eyes set so wide and shining. And the tantalizing little tilt of your nose — That forgetting business may take me years, Tolly — till I'm a mighty old man."

"Now let's tell 'sad stories of the death of kings,' " Tolly quoted huskily when she had blown her nose.

Their way led through the Great Smoky National Park, and was a twisting, turning climb through the

197

bright colors and among the mountains that diminished to a blue distance.

"These Cherokees," Rich said once, as they passed through a village lined with shops where Indian handicrafts were spread for sale, "they have had it worse than we have —"

"That doesn't make it any better for us," Tolly replied automatically, and they returned to their silences.

She was feeling by turns weighted down and empty as a toy balloon. To be scorned and hated as the mob had scorned and hated, and the waitresses and police and jailers — that had been horrible, but part of an old familiar pattern. And she knew that they were wrong.

Now she found herself judged by one of her own — and found wanting. And this made the third time in her young life. She summoned all her forces to resist those three, to prove to herself how deeply they had misjudged her.

It was late when they stopped in front of the Tolliver house, but light flooded from windows and door, and when Tolly ran in, followed by Rich, she was welcomed by a joyous tumult that seemed more than three persons could create.

Dabney jumped up and down like a mechanical toy, Papa was trying unobtrusively to get to Tolly ahead of Mama, and Mama was elbowing him out of the way and embracing her child.

Papa, thus detached, put out a hand to Rich, his eyes wet behind his glasses. "Mrs. Tolliver and I thank you, son, for looking after her. And Ellen — ?" His smiling face creased with worry.

"Pulse steady and no fever," Rich said with a subdued chuckle. "No, no — she's okay, sir."

"It won't take me two minutes to heat up the rest of the chicken and dumplings," Mama invited.

"Ma'am, it sounds wonderful. But Mother and Dad would say things to me if I didn't make haste over to Lady's and show them I haven't even a limb missing."

From the tail of her eye as she walked to the door with Rich, Tolly saw her mother grab Dabney so that they might go alone. She smiled bitterly. Wouldn't everyone be surprised to know that she was a maiden scorned?

But on the porch he said, "Would it be all wrong, after what I've said, to ask if I might kiss you good-by?"

She lifted her mouth to his.

"Good-by, Rich," she whispered. "It's been nice knowing you."

21

"Daughter, that's a fine lad you've annexed," Mr. Tolliver greeted her when she returned from the door.

"Except that I definitely have not annexed him." Tolly was blinking rapidly, though the lights were not bright.

"Well, he certainly seemed to be smitten." Mama's tone was reproachful. "And his mother says it's the first time he's come home for Thanksgiving. And he didn't stay for it this time. Took a Freedom Ride instead. What a Thanksgiving!"

"If he was ever smitten, he's well on the way to complete recovery. Good gracious!" Tolly broke off when her eyes refused to hold back the tears. "This burn on my neck does hurt like the dickens. Will you look at it, Mama?"

All attention was swung away from Rich as Mama clicked her tongue in alarm at the angry redness of the wound. Without more words she telephoned to Dr. Lincoln and, finding him at home, sent Tolly and her father to his office, which was in his house.

They were back inside the hour, Tolly comforted by clean dressings and fortified with antibiotics.

"How I shall sleep!" she said, stretching luxuriously

and stopping midway as she looked at the clock. "Heavens! I haven't called Mather. If it were anyone else I'd say it was way too late, but —" She grabbed the instrument and dialed the familiar number.

"Shall I come over in the morning?" she asked, hesitant because she wondered how her president was feeling about her prolonged absence. The reply was cheering. Indeed they would be looking for Tolly. They had got along reasonably well, but would be glad to have her back.

When her father drove with her onto the campus early next morning, Tolly felt an unexpected joy and peace. The sun kindled the long line of crape myrtles to a shimmering flame. It was a beautiful place to be, and its warmth and love seemed to reach out and enfold her. Tolly had heard people say that Mather girls were different. Perhaps this shine rubbed off on them, making them stand straighter, speak more softly, carry themselves with more dignity.

Her own unexpected appreciation expressed itself in her greeting to Gabe, who was the first student she met after her father drove away.

"Well, Gabe! How is everything with you?"

"It — it just fine, Miss Tolly," he stuttered.

"I may have a little leisure —" Somehow Tolly had to waste no time about this. "Want a little help, Gabe? After the last class today?"

Instead of beaming with happiness, the pixy face so far above her seemed disturbed, mouth sagging, eyes blinking. "Miss Tolly, you too good. But this afternoon I already promise —"

Tolly hastened to relieve his embarrassment. "Oh, another time will do as well, Gabe. Even better, far as I'm concerned."

The next person she met was Rosabelle, and her welcome was as unexpected as Gabe's, her look cool, almost hostile.

"Why, Rosabelle, aren't you feeling well?"

"I've been feeling fine, Miss Tolliver. But was I mistaken in thinking you shoved Gabriel Vesey off on me?"

Tolly gave an astounded laugh. "Shoved, Rosabelle?"

"Well, I've been working like mad on the poor gink, Miss Tolliver, and he's got something, he really has. And you'd think I was giving him diamonds, he's so grateful. But I'd be no competition for—"

"Rosabelle! That is quite enough." She could not let a student speak so to her, even if the student was only a year younger than she. But when Rosabelle leaned up against a wall and buried her face in her arms, Tolly's official manner melted.

"You little goon," she said gently, "I don't want your Gabe. You go on with your coaching. I won't interfere."

They stood so, Rosabelle's face still hidden, Tolly awkwardly patting and smoothing her. "Look," Tolly said with a small laugh, "the way I'm massaging you anybody'd think you had a shoulder out of joint."

"And it was only my nose," Rosabelle gulped, emerging from the seclusion of her arms. "I'm ashamed, Miss

Tolly. I guess I've been looking too far ahead. About Gabe. I've been thinking I might help him through college and maybe a professional school. Fixing hair. There's something about Gabe. When you think that he never even heard of Shakespeare—"

"There's something wonderful about you, Rosabelle," Tolly said warmly. "You aren't a bit afraid to involve your precious self —"

She felt humble as she sat before her first class that morning. It was a class that Gabe was in, and she detained him as he passed her desk, saying, "I see I can give that bit of spare time to someone else, Gabe. Flora — I've neglected Flora — and Rosabelle is tops, isn't she?"

As he flashed her a shy smile she noticed the new confidence in Gabe's bearing, the new poise of his head. A few days with the right girl — for the girl a few days with the right boy —

She shivered as if the mild fall day had turned chill. It had taken her years to learn who was the wrong boy, but Rich had needed only a few weeks to know that she was the wrong girl.

She forced herself to concentrate on the class. The thin, poor background of some of them, as Rosabelle had suggested, made it hard for them to grasp the poem they were asked to discuss. Theirs was such blank darkness, Tolly thought.

But some of these lifted to her face eyes that held a flicker of new light. It might be the flame of a candle or a torch, blown by adverse winds. But it held hope.

Gabe stopped again at her desk on his way out. He struck the wood with the flat of his palm and threw back his head in a laugh of pure delight. "Miss, I always think poetry was foolishment. But, you know, I'm beginning to get the hang of it. It means something," he announced, as if at an electrifying discovery. "This fellow here is trying to make us feel something that's kind of too big to get into words!"

Tolly was nodding and smiling, but Gabe was too full of his discovery to wait for her response. "My old grandpa, he always say reading and writing spoil black folks. He say we got the true wisdom, what the sun, moon, and stars teach us, and the tides, and the earth and its critters. And the witch doctors, with their good signs and their bad signs to guide us. But now I'm gwine try to make it clear to him that the books have wisdom, likewise."

The day was busy, and Tolly used any intervals to answer questions about the Freedom Ride.

"That little bit of an Ellen!" one of the teachers exclaimed. "When she was here at Mather she looked as if she belonged in kindergarten. So pretty and soft you wanted to pick her up and cuddle her."

"But there's a lot to her besides eyes and dimples," Tolly said. "Ellen's smart."

"Of course. Otherwise she wouldn't have been picked out of the junior class for early college entrance. Oh, she's smart."

"I always imagine Ellen married to a professional man and living up North," Tolly said, glowing at the dream of a lovely Ellen, with a husband something like Rich and in a house something like a Fisk professor's.

The thoughts continued in the back of her mind during the remainder of the day's classes and when she went to the Sales House to help. With Christmas in the offing and crisp nights and mornings warning of winter, the Sales House was doing a rushing business, and Mrs. Adams, who was waiting on customers, looked tired but unusually happy.

"Who left you a million dollars?" Tolly asked her.

"It's Ichabody." Mrs. Adams motioned backward.

There, to be sure, in his improvised pen, sat Ichabod, clean as if polished. At Tolly's approach, he squared his mouth in a howl, and stretched demanding arms toward his new mother. She laughed out exuberantly as she scooped him up on her hip and went on counting out her customers' nickels and dimes.

"Oh, how much work he must make you!" Tolly protested.

"He does!" Mrs. Adams agreed delightedly. "And I didn't know how badly I needed to be needed by someone of my own," she added, as the child dropped his curly head on her shoulder and contentedly thrust his thumb into his mouth.

"But his sister?" Tolly inquired. "Did it just about break her heart — the separation?"

" 'Melia?" Mrs. Adams asked, tucking her head down

as if to count better. "Why, way it turned out, I took 'Melia, too. We've applied for adoption papers. And she purely loves school. Tell you all about it later, Tolly. Have to mind what I'm doing."

The nickels and dimes were being exchanged for a pair of men's trousers and a stack of newspapers and bright magazine covers. Mrs. Adams tied them stoutly, and an old man gripped one bundle by the cord while the old woman with him, smiling and nodding delightedly, thrust her frail, knotted fingers under the twine on the other. "Now us kin trim the house fo' Christmas," she said, curtsying.

"So that's why they wanted the papers," Tolly said when they had gone out. "I couldn't think what for."

Mrs. Adams shook her head amusedly. "A few years ago half the customers wanted papers. Now people like that are the exception rather than the rule."

"My goodness," Tolly thought aloud, "how will Aunt Emmeline get her place prettied up for Christmas? Wonder if I couldn't get some of the kids to go on a work party —"

Dr. Eloise was well pleased with her idea. "I wouldn't put it past Aunt Emmeline," Tolly said darkly, "to do a little climbing herself if there was no other way —" and plans went forward for a work party the first Saturday in December, though it would mean hurrying home for basketball games that evening.

Tolly had no difficulty recruiting helpers: Rosabelle and Jenniedeane, the little kneel-in girl, and Flora, Gabe and Claude and Melom. Tolly wondered how industrious they would be. Melom admitted that he was going for the party rather than the work, to witness another of America's folkways. It was Flora who seemed likely to accomplish most. She was tiptoe with eagerness, and the face that so often fell into dull somberness was sparkling today.

"Flora," Tolly asked curiously, "what is making you so extra chipper? Or is that too inquisitive of me?"

Flora looked quickly at the others, but they were busy with their own plans. "Oh, Miss Tolly!" she gurgled, fervently clasping her hands, "I wasn't going to say anything until it was sure, but Dr. Andrews has recommended me to a big school of nursing in Minnesota. They wrote, offering scholarships. And the nurse, she said such good things—" Flora laughed tremulously, and carefully smoothed her smooth skirt.

"Oh, now, tell teacher!"

"Well, she said I was — the best nursing material she'd seen in a long time. — And we ought to get word from them any day."

"Congratulations!" Tolly said, patting her, but at the same time feeling a little anxious. She should have been working hard with that reading whenever there was a spare moment.

Somewhat to Tolly's surprise, the old St. Helena fashion of elaborately decorating the houses for the long Christmas holiday was new to all seven, and even she herself had to consult her father and mother and Aunt

Emmeline about some of the fine points. It was another example of the changes that had come to the islands since bridges and causeways had connected them with each other and the mainland.

Papa drove his plum-colored car filled with students across those bridges, and Claude had been able to borrow a jeep from a buddy in the Marine Corps and take Melom and the supplies. They had pooled their resources and bought boxes of cookies and packages of Koolaid. — "No kind of party," Gabe expressed the general feeling, "lessen you got eats." They had plenty of newspapers, too, as well as magazines with bright covers and advertisements.

The newspapers, Tolly explained to her forces, served two purposes: they made the walls clean and neat and also insulated them from the sharp, damp winds of winter.

All the way over, the heavy old car seemed to rock with laughter and song, while Papa's gold-rimmed spectacles reached a new high in twinkling and glittering, his smile a new golden glow. Claude and Melom and the jeep had passed them on the way and then had to wait for directions, but soon they were all crowding into Aunt Emmeline's cabin, and quieting their nonsense long enough to respond politely to introductions to her.

As soon as they had "made their manners," and ensconced Aunt Emmeline in her rocker, they set to work with the newspapers and the paste Aunt Emmeline had made.

Starting at the top, they would cover last year's dingy yellowed papers with clean, fresh layers.

Gabe could easily reach the highest point while standing flat-footed on the floor. — "Isn't he the most!" Rosabelle crowed admiringly. Even Claude had to balance precariously on one of the stools to match Gabe's performance, while Rosabelle and Flora stood on the only chairs, and Tolly leaped lightly to a table to do her part, first spreading newspaper over it because of Aunt Emmeline's careful cleanliness.

When the highest rows were pasted on, Tolly called a halt and laid out colored magazine covers and pages. "Look!" she said triumphantly, "Aunt Emmeline, you can have a frieze all the way round. Jenniedeane and Flora, this is your dish, because you're such little dolls."

At that, Flora went to work with even more of a will, cutting, pasting, placing, with the neat efficiency that seemed built into her. There would be one nurse who would roll her patient over onto a clean sheet without a jolt or a twinge, Tolly thought admiringly.

The cabin was soon banded about with a frieze at low eye height, exotic fruit salads, fruit pies, cakes, and legs of lamb alternating with rosy children, delectable babies, and high-chroma young men and women cooking over back-yard grills, driving, or water skiing.

"Want I should take down theseyere barrel hoops for you to fix up?" Gabe offered, and leaped on the table and did so, the hoops hanging high, to avoid the heads below.

Tolly pulled off the smoky old newspaper fringes and replaced them with new ones that Aunt Emmeline had cut. Tied to the rafters again, the hoops became lovely, shimmering chandeliers, swaying and rustling in every breeze.

"It's time," Tolly cried, "for us to take a breather."

Aunt Emmeline had been blessed with a good well, one which Uncle Doctor pronounced safe. The boys drew fresh, cold water, and the girls made Koolaid, pouring it into the bright paper cups they had brought. The students sat around on stools and floor, leaving the rocker for Aunt Emmeline and the chair for Tolly, who was having too good a time to take it.

While they gloated over their half-done handiwork, Tolly clutched at her hair. "The bluing for the frames and shutters! It completely dropped out of my mind. Our people," she explained to the ignorant nonislanders, "trim their windows and doors in blue. To keep out the lightning and evil spirits," she added with intense solemnity. "And I forgot to bring any."

"Honey chile," Aunt Emmeline said, "you look in yonder cupboard. Aun' Emmeline's always got bluing."

Tolly did so. "With that problem solved," she said, "I can enjoy some more cookies and Koolaid. If you're half starved, they look like a feast."

"Then I'm half starved," Gabe declared.

Perhaps sitting cross-legged on the cabin floor had swept Gabe back into the past so close behind him.

He smacked appreciative lips, scooped up a handful of cookies as the plate was passed again, and crowded them into his mouth.

"Hmmm," said Rosabelle, breaking off a dainty bite of hers.

Gabe was not slow on the uptake. He swallowed with such desperate haste that he coughed and strangled and sent cooky crumbs spraying into the air. And he compounded the offense by vigorously scratching first one shoulder and then the other.

"Hmmm!" Rosabelle repeated.

"Rosy Bell," Melom put in gravely, "scratching is completely natural to the very young. We, as adults, feel acutely only through our fingertips. The very young have fingertips over the entire body."

"Oh, go on!" Claude scoffed.

"Fact. Biology," Melom responded.

"No younger than the rest of you," Gabe muttered feebly.

"Melom, you learn more than all of us put together," Tolly said.

"It isn't Melom's brain that's lazy," Rosabelle teased.

Melom's eyes flashed at her, only half amused. "In my country men's work and women's is never the same. To be sure, I have seen the missionary men help their wives when needed — menial work. But they were white. However —"

With one fluid motion he sprang to his feet, seized a

rag that had been used as a paste brush, swiped it lavishly across a strip of newspaper, and leaped onto a stool.

Crrrash! the frail old wood shattered under his chunky weight, and only agile footwork saved him from falling.

Smiling composedly, he resumed his place on the floor. "The *mores* of my native land were too strong for me. It was not to be. Madame, I ask your pardon. It will be my great pleasure to fetch you a new stool," he said to Aunt Emmeline.

They finished their refreshments, Flora swept out the crumbs, Gabe — snorting — gathered up the broken stool and carried it to the woodpile, and the work began again.

"Miss Tolliver, she like to toil," groaned Gabe, rubbing his back with exaggerated gestures of pain.

"I'll like the results," Tolly corrected, "when we get the insides of the shutters covered — and the blue on."

It was a pity Rich could not see her now, she thought, in the jeans she had worn to climb around in — which Aunt Emmeline would have wanted to forbid, a few years ago — and with her head tied up in a bandanna and her hands crisscrossed with scratches. Wouldn't he have to admit that she was willing to do more for her people than some of the sentimental ones who were forever crying over them?

They were all tired by the time they had finished and Papa, who had been back and waiting for an hour, announced that they couldn't much more than get home for dinner. Papa drove right up to the speed limit, and

Claude, who had been invited to dinner, a little faster, and they had a scant few minutes to wash hands and faces, change clothes, smooth hair and get into the dining hall while the evening grace was being sung.

"Thou are great and Thou art good,
And we thank Thee for this food —"

Tolly liked the soaring young voices. She liked everything until later that night, just before the basketball games, when a hesitant knock sounded at her door. Stepping lightly across the room to open it, she stood astonished.

Flora was standing there, an entirely different Flora from the one who had bubbled her good news to Tolly that noon. This Flora had wilted, and her eyes were big with pain.

"Why, Flora!" Tolly stammered, "have you had bad news?"

Dry sobs kept back any words the girl might have been trying to say, and Tolly drew her gently into the room, pushed her down into a chair, closed the door.

"Now what is it, dear?" she asked, taking a small, limp hand in hers as she crouched beside her.

Flora gulped. "The letter came." She moved her head like a creature in pain. "They say — I may have the scholarship — if I fill out — the papers — good."

Tolly waited, catching her breath.

"Miss Tolly — I cain't. I don' know how to read it good enough — I don't know how to write it —" She stared at the older girl with tragic, desperate eyes.

Tolly swallowed back tears and steadied her voice with an effort. "Oh, Flora, we'll work harder than ever! I can give you more time —"

"It too late," the girl demurred. "I lose my big chance. Seem like I got most ever'thing but words. Just words."

It was then that Dr. Eloise called up to Tolly from the foot of the stairs. "A long-distance call for you, Tolly. You can take it in my room if you like."

"Thank you, Dr. Eloise. I'll be right down," Tolly answered. "Do you want to wait for me up here, Flora?" she asked the hopeless little creature who was rising from the chair. "Or we can talk later — Oh, Flora, I'll help all I can —"

"You too good, Miss Tolly. But thisyere was my chancet." She stumbled ahead of Tolly down the steep stairs and uttered a barely audible "Good night" as she went out the door.

Shaken by Flora's grief and by a dark doubt of what this long-distance call could be, Tolly followed her own gentle tapping into the president's room. The president was on the point of vanishing through another door, a half-dozen pompoms in her hand.

She paused, waving the pompoms. "I'm off to the games," she called. "You might come after you've finished with your call."

Automatically Tolly smiled and nodded as she took up the earpiece. Who could it be? Her parents? No — she had seen Papa two hours ago.

"Hello," she said into the mouthpiece.

"Is this Miss Tolliver?"

"Yes, this is she." Oh, hurry! hurry!

"Here's your party. Go ahead."

"Tolly! Oh, Tolly!"

It was Ellen's voice, in a great burst of relief — or despair?

"Yes, yes, it's Tolly. Baby, what's the matter?"

No answer except a childlike sob and sniffle.

"Ellen! Baby! Tell sister. You haven't flunked out?"

"No. No. Though I might. But the way you looked at me — after that Freedom Ride — I thought maybe you already guessed —"

Tolly clutched at the earpiece as if it would hold her up, and dropped into the chair which she had so far disregarded. She was staring incredulously into the phone. "Ellen — Ellen Tolliver! You can't mean —"

"But I do mean it," Ellen wailed. "And, after all, what's so awful about it — ?"

"You mean to say you're married? Ellen, when on earth — ?"

"Soon as we came back to Fisk in September. And you've got to break it to them, Tolly. I don't want Mama fainting on the floor when Orbert and I come home for Christmas." While Tolly tried to bite back the anger that came rushing to her lips, Ellen went on. "Orbert will have to get a job. Unless we can coax his folks over to our side. They're so mad at him. I thought maybe Papa —"

215

Tolly's whirling senses had steadied enough so that she could speak reasoningly. "Ellen, you're only sixteen. You couldn't get married."

Her sister's laugh flicked Tolly on the raw, and not till later did she think that it was not a happy laugh. "But I did. It may not be legal, but it's certainly a fact."

Through the petted, babyish voice of Ellen Tolly seemed to hear Flora's hopeless one: "Too late — this-yere was my chancet."

Tolly spoke rapidly, harshly into the phone, thankful that there was no one within earshot, and she could speak the thoughts that demanded utterance. "Well, all I can say is that you are even more selfish than I knew. And senseless, losing all the wonderful opportunities given you. Here Papa and Mama have gone without so much, just to give you the best education — oh, Ellen!"

Was it a little, gasping sob that Tolly heard again? The operator's voice cut between them. "Your three minutes are up, ma'am. Will you deposit — ?"

"Oh, I haven't it," Ellen quavered.

Tolly slammed the phone back on its cradle and stalked from the room and upstairs.

22

It was too late to go home that evening, but Miss James, a teacher who had been there during Tolly and Ellen's student days, offered to drive her home the following afternoon. On the way over, Tolly discussed the problem with her.

The teacher shook her head, her strong, patient face sorrowful. "Times are so changed. But this is not a cause for shame, Tolly; only for disappointment. Will it be better to tell your parents tonight only that Ellen is married? Has been married for several months?"

"I suppose so. Give them time to get used to all their lost labor. You sacrifice and work for years, and then the one you've worked for throws it all away —"

"Of course, though, the person to feel saddest about is little Ellen. Oh, it was reckless of Ellen, but all society, including us, has contributed to her mistake. Poor child!"

And, by the same reasoning, poor Sojer? Memories of the goodness in him crowded back on Tolly, memories of his strong face, wrung with sorrow and shame; memories of herself, shucking him off like a torn glove —

Maybe Rich was right about her.

As her face twisted out of control, she dropped her head, clasping herself tightly with crossed arms, eyes pressed shut against the tears that oozed beneath her lids.

"Don't take it so hard, dear." Miss James's voice deepened with sympathy. "It isn't too late for Ellen, with all of you showing her that she can go on, only losing a little time. Don't let her lose her sense of dignity, of worth, Tolly."

His dignity and worth. His strength and fineness. Please keep it from being too late, God. And tell me what to do. And tell me how to make this hurt least for Papa and Mama.

When she came in, smiling as if her visit were only a chance surprise, she felt that Someone really was helping her. "I heard from Ellen," she said, "the little rascal. She asked me to break it gently about her coming home week after next."

"You don't mean she isn't coming," cried Mama, "after our fixing up your room in her favorite shade of pink —"

Papa took off his spectacles and polished them on his coat sleeve, suspiciously eying Tolly.

"Oh, she's coming. She's bringing Orbert along."

"Oh, man!" Dabney shrilled. "Why couldn't she leave that lightweight out of it?"

"Don't call your brother-in-law a lightweight," Tolly advised.

Papa sighed and replaced his spectacles. Mama

clutched at her heart and backed to a chair and dropped into it. Dabney screeched, "Oh, for crying out loud! How does he come to be my brother-in-law?"

"They were married last September," Tolly said crisply.

A ring of the doorbell took Dabney on the run to admit Miss James.

"Good evening to you all. Sorry to break up a family conclave, but the wind is rising, and we should get to the Main."

"But what — ? How — ?" Mama clutched at Tolly's sleeve as Tolly bent to kiss her.

"Mama, I don't know whether it was a civil ceremony, or religious. And I don't know how the child convinced anyone she was of age. You'll have to phone Ellen — no, better wait till week after next, when she can tell you everything."

Hurriedly she kissed her father, aimed a kiss at Dabney, who dodged it, and followed the teacher to her car, the family close on her heels and still asking questions. When at last they could draw away from the Tolliver house, Tolly and Miss James exchanged significant glances.

"Tolly, as far as I could guess, you did nobly."

"But what next?"

"Well, obviously, your sister and the baby —" The baby! — "And the young husband, too, must be considered."

"Suppose if Papa and Mama kept Ellen there till fall,

219

that darn' boy's folks might relent and put him on through Fisk — ?"

"Might or might not. But other young husbands manage without parental help. And Ellen —"

"Ellen is fine, underneath. We've spoiled her."

"Yes, you worst of all," Miss James assented.

Tolly flinched, as if from an unexpected cold shower. "Anyway, she has the stuff, in spite of this piece of idiocy."

"Yes, the best persons sometimes make the most tragic mistakes. It's what they do afterward that counts. And there's where a helping hand —"

"Instead of a foot kicking them deeper." Tolly spoke heavily.

As soon as they had fought their way home against a rising wind, Tolly uncertainly thrust out those helping hands.

First she wrote to Ellen, telling her that she was sorry she had been so cross, but she loved her little sister so much — And Ellen could count on her to help any way she could —

Then she wrote to the young Core attorney. It might not do a speck of good, but today she had known with clear conviction that she had made no great effort before, and that she had tried to believe that the Freedom Rider with the swinging arm was not Sojer.

Would the attorney put this personal advertisement in a paper in the Alabama town where the Freedom Riders had been jailed, and where she had seen the young man who resembled an old friend? Would he insert it also in the nearest big newspaper, one with wide circulation, and in other likely papers, as many as the enclosed money order would buy?

Sojourner T. Pratt, attention! Please write or come to J.E.T., at St. Helena or at Mather School.

If it was Sojer, under an assumed name, whom she had seen beaten that day — If he happened to see her advertisement —

If these improbables came to pass, surely Sojer would understand. Surely he would read between the lines, "Whatever has happened, Sojer, you still matter to J.E.T. She still knows that you are fine, and that you have a future. She still —"

Reaching this point, Tolly flung herself face down across her bed. She should have added, "if you can forgive her."

When at last she rolled over and from swollen eyes contemplated the ceiling, she felt that she had wept away not only her breath but much of the hard coldness which had gripped her, and which Flora's tragedy had begun to thaw.

And now the days before the Christmas vacation were filled to the brim for Tolly. The school celebration was always a great occasion, and Tolly helped with the pageant as well as continuing to teach night school. She also made Christmas gifts, concocting a sock doll for Ichabod and new clothes for a treasured doll of her own for Amelia, and devising for Aunt Emmeline and the family presents that could be squeezed out of what she had left from her advertising.

"I hope I'm not overstepping," she apologized, when Dr. Andrews found her sweeping in one of the dormitories. "Jenniedeane is rehearsing for the pageant, and I said I'd do their room this once. But I know that having to take care of their rooms and help with the general housework is one of the school's strong points," she hastened to add.

Dr. Andrews's laugh rang out. "You didn't feel that way when you were a student here, did you?"

"Kid stuff," Tolly deprecated. "I thought it was taking time from my lofty brain. Toplofty. Didn't see that part of the girls hadn't the remotest idea that there was a proper way to make a bed, or that they shouldn't sweep the dirt under it. Obviously the rules must apply to those who don't need them, in order to reach those who do."

"Well, however that may be, you're a dynamo, Tolly. More than ever these last few days. Somehow you're different."

She felt different. I was all mixed up, she thought. I didn't throw myself into the work here — just reached in from outside as if I were an observer.

It was a wonderful campus, with almost everyone really caring about everyone else. There was harmony between the Negro teachers and the white ones. Tolly found herself forgetting that they were white, and forgiving them when she did remember. They were people.

There was light here, light in the darkness. A thousand candles. Torches in the wind and dark.

On Thursday, December 21, Papa came to take Tolly home. Papa looked several years older and smiled less readily. But his leg was doing well, and he got around with a walking cast and a cane.

"Mama has taken on almost continuously, daughter. Who can blame her? She confidently expected a great future for Ellen. And neither of us, I must confess, feel any warm enthusiasm for the young man." He shook his head so sorrowfully that the woman waving to him from a roadside garden skittered out to her gate and peered after him.

"Have you heard from Ellen, Papa?"

"A note or two. No real communication. Has she divulged more to you?"

"Since the phone call I haven't had even a note, though I wrote to her at once. She is put out with me because I scolded her when she told me."

She had received no answer to her advertisement, either, except a businesslike acknowledgment from the Core attorney, listing the newspapers that were running her personal. This time she had resolved not to watch for an answer so early. Yet she was beginning to feel, with a heavy heart, that if there were any response it would come soon —would have come sooner than this.

Ellen and Orbert arrived the next day. Mama clasped Ellen to her breast and swayed to and fro with her, Ellen scrambling on her absurd little high heels to keep her footing. Finally Mama extended a cold hand to the young husband. "Mr. Orbert, I can only say that you have given us an unhappy surprise."

To this warm welcome Orbert responded with a feeble smile.

"Ellen, here's your big sister," Tolly reminded her.

"And I suppose she's going to bawl me out the way she did over the phone." Ellen's eyes were both wary and sulky.

Tolly laughed shortly. "Let bygones be bygones, sister. Today is today." But one thing she would not do: she would no longer call Ellen "baby," she resolved, as she looked across the silky head which had deposited itself on her breast, and met her father's sorrowful eyes.

Ellen, in that strong, warm clasp, gave way to feelings perhaps long pent. Her body shook with sobs, and her small, hot hands clutched at her sister.

"I — I'm so scared," she whispered. "I — don't like it."

"There, there, baby," Tolly whispered. "Sister will help you work things out."

Next morning Orbert and Ellen took Tolly and Dabney to visit Aunt Emmeline. The little convertible was a help, Tolly admitted, since Papa was busy with pastoral calls, Mama still driving for him. As usual they took food, and anything else that might give Aunt Emmeline pleasure.

"And this the boy our little Ellen marry with!" Aunt

Emmeline greeted them. "Ellen, he carry his head pridefully. Mind you rule 'm good, girl!" She laughed, and gave Orbert a pat on the shoulder, but Tolly was sure the old eyes were less than happy, much as Aunt Emmeline relished a romance. "Yo' baby sister, Tolly, when it time to grow up, she grow up. You wait and see."

And when they said they must go, Aunt Emmeline lifted her face, eyes closed. "Thank you, Lawd Jesus," she chanted softly, "this old sheep was all ready to come home and lay down beside them still waters. But if it pleases you I stay, then I stay, Lawd. And I thank you for these young ones, dear as if they was of my own flesh. Bless them and keep them and make thisyere new family strong and happy and good. Amen."

Opening her eyes, Tolly saw the telltale wetness on Aunt Emmeline's face, and dabbed furtively at her own. The silence was broken by a curious sound that turned into an unconvincing cough. Tolly darted a surprised look at Orbert, the hard-boiled. He was drawing down his upper lip and blinking.

"Awful draft in here," he muttered belligerently.

Ellen made a childlike dive toward him and nestled in his arms, and they clung together, her head tucked under his chin and her eyes tight closed. They might conceivably make something of this rash marriage, Tolly thought — just conceivably.

"Isn't there something we can do for you, Aunt Emmeline?" Tolly asked. "Ellen and Orbert are going on to his folks for Christmas, but I'll be cooking, and so will

Mama. I'll bring you a loaf of the Christmas bread Papa likes so well, and anything else you'd enjoy. And don't go roasting a turkey!" she added with a laugh. "Remember you're having Christmas dinner with us."

23

Papa often said that Christmas was not quite so breathtaking as in his childhood. Then it crowned a year of hard work and the simplest pleasures with joy, praise, feasting, and fun.

It was still a gay time, with busy days of preparation. Much had already been done by Mama. Tolly, and Ellen, and Orbert before they set out for the drive to northern Virginia, went around lifting the waxed paper to sniff the fruit cakes that had been ripening for a month, and admiring the jellies and preserves and the mince pies in the freezer. Especially to please Papa, Mama had baked the molasses-sweetened bread that the islanders used always to break in luscious chunks for Christmas breakfast. For dinner, the center of interest would be the big turkey, stuffed to bursting with oysters.

The parsonage was unusually busy and bustling on the last day of the young couple's stay. Tolly was finding comfort in doing more for Ellen than could have been asked of her, and even showing some grudging kindnesses to Orbert. The washing machine swished and chattered over load after load of their clothes, and the iron in Tolly's grasp steamed its way across them all.

Mama put up a lunch ample for several meals, and sent to Orbert's family two of her mince pies, delicately brown and oozing richness. Finally Papa and Dabney lugged out the box Tolly had been packing with gorgeously wrapped presents and wedged it into the scant space left for it.

After both young people were in the car, Ellen pulled herself out again and ran to hug and kiss all her family except the determined Dabney. She came last to Tolly, and whispered, "Thank you, sis. You — you're somehow different."

But not different enough, Tolly thought with a shaken laugh. "You're different yourself, baby," she whispered.

"And so is Orbert — haven't you noticed? Tolly, we — we mean to make this work out, we really do." With another kiss, she pushed back into the crowded little car.

When they were gone, with much honking and waving, Tolly rushed back to her work. She had her rather meager gifts to wrap, making up for their meagerness with gay paper and ribbons saved from other years. And she had Christmas candy to make: pralines, with pecans from the big trees in their yard, benny candy, rich with sesame seeds, peanut brittle.

For once Dabney was willing to help, since he was allowed to scrape the kettles after he had beaten the creamy masses till they could be poured out.

"But why do you stick away the nicest pieces in every batch?" he demanded.

"It's just the ones I think might be his favorites —"

Tolly answered without thinking, and stopped abruptly.

"Whose favorites? Papa's? Seems like you'd be sure what Papa likes best. He likes 'em all."

Tolly's slip was safely passed over. She was silly to put aside the most luscious rounds and squares. And she could only guess that her favorites would be Sojer's. She was paying useless tribute to the past.

Next Christmas, some way, I'm coming to St. Helena. How often she had heard him say it, during their last semester at Fisk. Don't know how, but I'll come, Tolly — if you want me to.

Next Christmas at St. Helena. It reminded Tolly of the ever-repeated Jewish cry, "Next year at Jerusalem."

She had not known that Christmas, without him, would have moments of almost unbearable sadness. Was he many miles away? Or was he nowhere on earth?

"What are you thinking about?" Dabney asked pettishly, as she stood with spoon suspended above a bubbling, glossy chocolate lake.

"Right now I'm thinking it would be nice if you'd go out and get some holly, so we could make a wreath," Tolly said, pulling herself back to the present with an effort.

Two days later came Christmas Eve.

Papa met the postman as he tried to jam the cards and packages into the mailbox at the road. Papa had taken out a huge sack, and limped back with it dangerously full. Dabney, who had followed him with arms flailing, most inconveniently helped him carry it.

Tolly forced herself to stand watching when he dropped into a chair and began sorting out the few packages, the cards and the letters, which Dabney piled at the foot of the Christmas tree in the corner.

The packages were all accounted for. One was from Langston: candy, it looked like. Tolly's eyes leaped to each letter as Papa handed it to Dabney, straining to make out the handwriting. When he said, "That is all — and it is amply sufficient for two families, if you want my opinion," Tolly could not keep from reaching for the bag and turning it upside down, to make sure he had not missed the one important message.

Papa, Tolly and Dabney went early to do Christmas Eve chores for Aunt Emmeline and then take her to the Christmas Eve praise service. Later, the Lincolns would pick up Mama.

All the way to Aunt Emmeline's, Papa was murmuring snatches of his sermon. It was not the year for the big Mystery Play which St. Helena performed biennially. But this was a big night, too. With so many distractions, Papa said, he had not given the usual careful preparation to what he considered one of the important occasions of the year. His people seemed to think more about the true meaning of Christmas than most folks did. Yet did they feel deeply enough the wonder, the amazement of God's involving Himself with the poor miserable creatures he had made in his image?

Tolly studied him suspiciously when he brought out the word "involve," with which she had so quarreled.

"Papa, don't try to cover up. You're preaching at your own daughter."

"What's that?" Mr. Tolliver looked ahead with eyes innocently round. "Not many of them will get my point, perhaps. But it makes me tremble to think of it: God so great and me so little and no-account, and He not satisfied to stay outside and just put things into shape with a mighty Word. No, He had to get right into it through His own Son. And feeling as I do about you children, and how what hurts you hurts me worse — Almighty God, how much more Your love for your Son was — and how much more You hurt!"

The smoke from Aunt Emmeline's chimney rose as straight as a ruled line into the still evening air when they went hastening up her path. She was ready, even to the ancient black straw sailor hat perched atop her headcloth.

"Would it be too much to ask, Reverend —" she spoke hesitantly — "to put the little critter with his mother for the night?"

Papa nodded understandingly and went out. Aunt Emmeline still held the old belief that cattle, sheep, horses, and donkeys shared the Christmas rejoicing, and knelt in their stalls on Christmas Eve when the cocks crowed for "middle-night."

"Critter-babies," Aunt Emmeline was murmuring, "ought to be with their mothers then, same as people-babies."

Tolly banked the open fire as Aunt Emmeline had

taught her. Fire should be kept, for it was a precious thing, with a soul of its own — but not the cheap new fire men made with matches.

So at last they set out for the church. "It must have been more beautiful when it was in the praise house," Tolly thought aloud.

Aunt Emmeline's black hat and white coif nodded assent. "Befo' long them praise houses molder to dust."

The church area was thronged with all sorts of vehicles, but the minister's place had been saved for him, and Aunt Emmeline did not have far to walk. Papa came around to open the car door and help her out, and they started up the path, Dabney capering ahead, Papa on one side of the wisp of an old woman, Tolly on the other.

The stars seemed bigger and more mysterious tonight. Those singing stars and the laughing, talking crowds of people were part of a whole, and Tolly's heart swelled with wonder and longing.

Dabney came racing back, dodging around and between the entering throng. "Can't you shake a leg?" he demanded. "It's filling up fast. Annemmeline won't get far enough front to see —"

He stopped, and his mouth dropped open as he stared up into the darkness behind Tolly. Tolly turned her head to see what had caught his attention.

Her fingers dropped from Aunt Emmeline's arm. She turned all the way around, slowly, as if fearful of waking from a dream, and stood rooted, holding her breath.

Then — "Sojer — Sojer — Sojer!" she sobbed.

From some distance Aunt Emmeline was murmuring, "Evening, sir!" and Papa was saying, "Well, son, we welcome you. Daughter, we will go in. You two can follow."

He and Aunt Emmeline and Dabney melted away, Dabney's round, astonished eyes visible longest. Vague figures jostled Tolly and Sojer, standing unmindfully in the middle of the path. The vague figures emitted vague words, "Beg pardon," and "Evening, Tolly." She did not answer. These were characters in a blurred TV and only Sojer was real.

She put her two hands into his and they stood there, looking and looking. She could make out the broad brow, the flare of eyebrows, the gaunt cheeks, and, when the doorway was cleared and light poured out upon them, the livid scar from hairline to chin.

She said, "Why did you go away, Sojer? Under some other name?"

"I thought Pa wouldn't take it out on Ma so bad if I was gone. But more, I guess, it was like crawling away into the dark to hide the hurt."

"But the Freedom Ride — ?"

"It seemed like doing something again. Something real. I didn't know if you saw me, Tolly. — But one of the Fisk profs happened to come to the hospital while I was there, and he said he knew I could have another chance at Fisk. But I hadn't the heart, Tolly. Not until I saw your advertisement." His long, shuddering breath shook them both. "I promised to come this Christmas.

233

If you wanted me to. I gave it up. Then I saw the advertisement — Does it mean — for true? Tolly, a common
roustabout, not fitten —"

"Nothing common about you," Tolly sobbed. "You
are Dr. Pratt. Future tense, yes. But Dr. Pratt, for sure."

"Tolly, honey, you ever figure how old I'll be, after I
take another year at Fisk and from four to six at Meharry?
It's a long road I got to climb, Tolly honey, and I'll be
pushing thirty if I get to the top."

Pushing thirty. The phrase gave Tolly a pang, but she
answered without hesitation.

"It's a long road, yes. But two of us together. I can
probably be teaching at Mather till you're through, if I
take summer work toward a graduate degree. And then
— twenty-six and thirty isn't too old for marrying. And I
can still teach till you're established and doing all the
earning."

She made a sound halfway between a sob and a
chuckle. "Come to think of it, Sojer, you'd be pushing
thirty in six or seven years even if you didn't take the
medical course."

Sojer threw back his head and laughed. It was his old
laugh, undiminished and unscarred. It was rich and
whole and healing.

And at that moment a great burst of song rang from
the crowded church, the little organ and the voices of
men, women and children, all underscored by the puls-
ing tap of many feet:

"Go tell it on the mountain!"